KU-652-738

Raymond Haigh was born, educated and has lived in Doncaster, South Yorkshire, all his life. He is married with four children and six grandchildren. *Cripplehead* is his third crime novel featuring Northern private eye Paul Lomax.

CRIPPLEHEAD

Private eye Paul Lomax never wanted the case. Checking on errant wives wasn't his scene, but keeping an eye on Rex Saunders' ex-fashion-model wife, Mona, promised to be all profit and no pain. How was Lomax to know that foxy old Rex was keeping so many secrets? And then there was the problem of Lomax's budding relationship with the irrepressible Melody Brown. Taking the case didn't help the romance along, especially when Mona dumped her inhibitions. Now Mona is terrified by sickening threats and the local morgue is filling up fast. When a hit man moves in and the police don't want to know, Lomax and Mona find themselves on their own.

Books by Raymond Haigh
Published by The House of Ulverscroft:

COLDER THAN THE GRAVE

RAYMOND HAIGH

◆

CRIPPLEHEAD

Complete and Unabridged

ULVERSCROFT
Leicester

First published in Great Britain in 2004 by
Robert Hale Limited
London

First Large Print Edition
published 2005
by arrangement with
Robert Hale Limited
London

British Library CIP Data

Haigh, Raymond
    Cripplehead.—Large print ed.—
    Ulverscroft large print series: mystery
    1. Lomax, Paul (Fictitious character)—Fiction
    2. Private investigators—England—Fiction
    3. Detective and mystery stories
    4. Large type books
    I. Title
    823.9'14 [F]

    ISBN 1–84395–884–8

Published by
F. A. Thorpe (Publishing)
Anstey, Leicestershire

Set by Words & Graphics Ltd.
Anstey, Leicestershire
Printed and bound in Great Britain by
T. J. International Ltd., Padstow, Cornwall

This book is printed on acid-free paper

1

She broke the surface quite close to us. The sudden rush and swirl of water startled me. Dark hair, high forehead, huge dark eyes, generous mouth, tiny chin: she began to climb the steps. I could see tanned shoulders now, and the movement of her body was making her unrestrained breasts tremble beneath the shimmering gold of her bathing-suit. Slender waist curved out to rounded hips that were swaying as she rose from the water, exposing more and more of her endless legs. Her hands swept around the chromium rails and she stepped up on to the pool-side. She made Botticelli's Venus look like an old crone climbing out of a flooded dyke. I guess she was the most beautiful woman I've ever seen, before or since.

I heard him cough to attract my attention, but I didn't take my eyes off her. I couldn't. She was looking down at me, soft lips curved into a faint smile, beads of water glistening on smooth brown skin.

'This is my wife, Mona. Mona, this is a business associate of mine.'

I pushed myself out of the canvas chair,

1

extended a hand and grasped hers. It was cold and wet and felt as small as a child's.

'How do you do, Mr . . . '

'He's come about the new time-share flats in Marbella.'

Her husband said that hastily. I sensed he didn't want her to know my name, so I just smiled and said, 'How do you do, Mrs Saunders?'

She smiled right back. It was a radiant smile. It needed her eyes, her lips, the dimples in her cheeks to make it that good. It was just about the best thing I'd seen all year. When she said, 'Can I get you both a drink?' her voice was soft and refined, haunted by the faintest trace of a southern Irish accent.

'He can't stay long, and we've got some details to finalize. Could you leave us for a while, honey?'

'Of course,' she said.

He threw her a towel. She caught it, pressed it to her cheeks. Huge dark eyes looked at me over the folds of white cloth for a second, then she turned and sauntered towards the door that led to the hallway of the house.

I just stood there, watching the rise and fall of her hips, the liquid melting of movement into movement. Her hair hung to the small of her back and the swimsuit plunged even lower. Her tan swept, all the way down, in an unbroken tide.

She disappeared through the door. I sat down and turned towards him again. Amusement was creasing the corners of his eyes, softening the lines of his face. He'd been studying the effect his wife had had on me: he must have seen it a million times before.

I said, 'What's your problem, Mr Saunders?'

He took a cigar from his mouth and used it to point towards the door. 'She's my problem, Mr Lomax. Or at least, I think she might be.'

I eyed him steadily, took in the big features, the balding head, the pelt of sandy hair on his arms and chest, the paunch straining against the waistband of his gaudy cotton shorts. His face and neck and forearms were red and weather-beaten; the flesh of his body putty-coloured, smooth as a girl's. I guessed he'd be in his mid-fifties. I was looking at the flabby remnants of a big, powerful man.

He must have guessed what I was thinking, because his fleshy lips moved into a worldly smile and he said, 'I don't have to worry about that department, Mr Lomax. I can cope OK if I pace myself. In fact, I cope pretty damn well.' His voice was gruff and throaty, like a market-stall spieler's. You could have turned his Yorkshire accent on a lathe.

3

'And how can I help you with your problem, Mr Saunders?'

'I want her followed for a week, two weeks, maybe a month. I want an hour-by-hour report on where she goes, who she goes with, and what she does when she gets there. I want the works: every last detail.'

'Sorry,' I said, 'I don't tackle that kind of job. I mostly handle commercial work. I try and leave the domestic stuff to the outfits that specialize in it.' The faint echoes of my voice were whispering around the high ceiling.

He blew smoke across the pool, then scowled down at his cigar. 'I don't want a firm that specializes, I want someone I can trust. I'm told you're strong on integrity, that you're discreet. You've been very highly recommended to me, Mr Lomax.'

'May I ask by whom?'

'Palmer, Alan Palmer. He said you'd done a job for him. If he says you're the business, then you're the best.' He wedged the cigar into the corner of his mouth and wrapped his lips around it.

I stared at him some more. Shrewd eyes, almost hidden by folds of flesh, gazed right back. I considered his offer. I needed the cash but I needed the job like I needed a dose of athlete's foot. I carried scars from tangling with other people's personal problems, and that included Alan Palmer's. But I'd instinctively warmed to him. A small-town guy who'd journeyed a long way without picking up any pretensions: a guy who wouldn't expect you to pay to shake his hand. And that didn't make saying no any easier.

I worked my features into an apologetic expression and said, 'I'm sorry, Mr Saunders, but I really don't handle that kind of case.'

He grunted, rolled the cigar over and clamped it in his other cheek. He reached into a folder that lay on a low table beside his chair and withdrew a king-size chequebook. He took a ball-point and began to write, slowly and carefully.

I glanced down the pool. It was laid out in sweeping curves. I figured he must have roofed over a small lake and stuck fancy tiling all around it: buff, white, two tones of blue, all in whirling convoluted patterns. The atmosphere in there was warm and humid, permeated by the acrid tang of chlorine. Islands of ferns and yucca plants in stone troughs relieved the smooth harshness of the tiling, made the place look a little like a municipal hothouse. Golden September sunlight flooded in through tall arched windows that ran the length of one wall. Beyond, grass and shrubs and trees, arranged in the same natural curving way as the pool, were soaking

5

up the last of the fading summer warmth.

I heard paper tearing along a perforation and looked back at him. He reached forward and laid a cheque on my knee.

'If I want the best, I don't mind paying for it, Mr Lomax.'

I took the slip of paper, glanced down at the figures. He'd been generous way beyond extravagance. I glanced up at him. He was unloading a couple of inches of ash into a stone planting-trough set against the wall behind us.

'Like I said, Mr Saunders, I don't really care to handle this type of case.'

'Do this one for me,' he said throatily. There was a kind of resigned sadness in the set of his features, about the way he was slumped in the chair. The worry and pain that lurked behind his eyes said that something was eating him up pretty bad.

I was weakening. Things had never been so good I could afford to turn down an advance like that. And then pride began to assert itself. I didn't want him to think it was just a question of money with me, that I could be bought. So I said, 'OK, Mr Saunders, I'll take the case, but I won't take the cheque.' I reached over, dropped it on the table beside him, then began to give him details of my hourly rates.

He grinned at me. It was obvious he wasn't listening. He picked up the cheque, folded it a couple of times, then heaved himself clear of his chair and tucked it in my breast-pocket.

'Take it,' he said, in his hoarse spieler's voice. 'And if it only takes a couple of days, you can keep the change. If it takes longer than a couple of weeks, you can have some more of the same. But I want the facts, Mr Lomax. Don't shoot me a load of lies because you start fancying her yourself. Most of all, don't do a social-worker on me and hold things back because of what I might do or to keep a marriage together.'

His flabby bulk was close to my chair, his paunch almost hanging over me. I could feel the warmth of his body; smell his sweat. I shoved the chair back, rose to my feet and got his eye level below mine. We began to walk down the side of the pool. My footsteps echoed: his large bare feet made no sound. The water was flat and clear and still, like a block of glass.

'Is there anywhere that your wife goes on a regular basis?'

'Hairdresser's every Friday morning, some health and fitness place every Wednesday afternoon, a bridge club on Thursday evenings. Most other times she says she's going shopping. She does a lot of shopping.'

'What makes you think she could be fooling around?'

He shrugged. 'Just a feeling.'

'Nothing more than that?'

'No, nothing.' He eyed me shrewdly. 'Are you married, Mr Lomax?'

'I was once.'

'Divorced?'

I looked away from him, across the flat expanse of water. 'No, widower.'

'I'm sorry.'

'Don't be, it was a long time ago.'

'Young, was she?'

I raised an eyebrow. It was unusual for people to probe, and it wasn't something I cared to talk about. 'She was almost thirty.' I let that echo around the high ceiling for a few seconds, then added, 'My daughter was six. Some arsehole of a joyrider hit them head on.'

He pretended to clear his throat, maybe wishing now he'd never asked the question. 'Well,' he coughed, 'even so, you'll know what I mean when I say you can tell when something's wrong, when a woman's gone cold on you and started pretending.'

'Or when she's not bothering to pretend any more,' I said.

He gave a wry chuckle. 'Yeah, maybe that's it.'

'Can I ask what you do for a living?'

He brightened. I guess he'd been dying to tell me.

'Sure. I'm in the construction business. Specialize in the luxury end, where there's always money. Domestic swimming pools, lavish refurbs. I'm moving into time-share flats now. Not tatt: high-quality stuff. And no small-print scams, either. Punters pay their cash and they get a good deal.'

'Has your wife got a car?'

He nodded. 'White two-seater Mercedes.' He gave me the registration number. I scribbled it down on the back of his cheque.

'And there's only one way out from your lane on to the main Barfield Road?'

'That's right. The other way ends up in a rutted track that leads to a farm. When will you start?'

'Over the next couple of days. It's best to give your wife a little time to start forgetting I've been here.'

When we reached a door that led into the garden, he turned a corroded key and dragged it open. It protested a little. I guess they hardly ever used it.

He said, 'Do you need a photo?'

I shook my head. 'I don't think I'll forget what your wife looks like, Mr Saunders.'

The fleshy mouth pulled into a grin, and

there was no jealousy or rancour in his voice as he said, 'Yeah, you were staring hard enough and she was showing you plenty. I just hope there's not some stinking little turd she's showing everything to.'

He took a last pull at his cigar and threw the butt into the shrubbery. Smoke began to drift out through big, hairy nostrils. He eyed me steadily for a while, then said softly, 'She's beautiful, Mr Lomax. When I look at her I just melt inside, she's so beautiful. And she's got class; maybe too much class for a guy like me. Sometimes she makes me feel kind of edgy and uncomfortable.' The gravelly voice tailed off, and his eyes left mine and became sightless as he gazed into the distance. Presently he sniffed, pulled his shoulders back, and made his voice threateningly urgent as he said, 'Get it sorted for me, Mr Lomax. And, like I said, don't hold anything back. There's a lot hanging on this. I've got some big decisions to make.'

He held out a hand the size of a frying-pan. I grasped it. It was soft. I guess it was some time since he'd used it to hold a shovel. His handshake was firm, but not challenging. There seemed to be real warmth in it.

'And you'll be discreet, won't you, Mr Lomax? I wouldn't want Mona to realize what's going on. Perhaps I'm just imagining

10

things, and what she doesn't know won't hurt her.'

'Sure,' I told him. 'I'll be discreet.'

'And you'll report everything?'

'Every lousy little detail. That's what you're paying me for, Mr Saunders, and that's what you'll get.'

2

The drive back to Barfield took less than fifteen minutes. I eased the old 3.5-litre Jaguar into a parking slot near the market-place, then headed up the rise to the office. 'Office' is a couple of frowsty attic rooms in a converted Georgian town house that faces the parish church. Sunlight was making the brass nameplates along the terrace sparkle brighter than a streetwalker's smile; the glorious Indian summer looked all set to run through into October.

I climbed worn entrance steps, collected the mail from the box behind my slot and glanced through Melody's reception window as I crossed the lobby.

Miss Melody Brown is the blue-eyed blonde who owns and manages a typing and photocopying agency that takes up most of the ground floor. On a friendly and strictly no-charge basis, she does my typing, handles reception and keeps an eye on the office when I'm out, which is most of the time.

Three or four girls were gazing into computer screens, their fingers busily pecking away at keyboards. Melody wasn't in view, so

I trudged on up the stairs, rounded the landing and stepped into the tiny waiting-room. Only the pile of dog-eared magazines was mine. The wood-grained Formica coffee table and half-dozen red plastic chairs were rented from some office equipment outfit; the previous government surplus items had been snatched by the bailiffs. I figured they might as well snatch someone else's gear next time.

I clattered across dingy brown linoleum that had been nailed down when the place was built, unlocked the inner door and sauntered through. Sunlight had given papers, upholstery, threadbare carpet and ancient dust a good baking. The place was as fragrant as a rat-catcher's bag.

I crossed over to the window, raised the bottom sash, then got behind the desk and began to open the mail. A couple of small cheques, a final rate demand, and an invitation to have my unwanted leg and facial hair painlessly removed. I pocketed the cheques and distributed the rest amongst the piles on the desk. Who knows, I might need a few leg hairs removing one day.

Footsteps pattered through the waiting-room, crockery rattled on a tray, and Melody was coming across the office towards me. I smiled. It was an autonomic response to pure pleasure. She was wearing a blouse made from some misty black material patterned with opaque black polka dots. Its collar was wide, sleeves full, cuffs long and tight like her crimson skirt. Waves of blonde hair were brushing her shoulders, and big blue eyes contrasted vividly with a golden tan. It had been a good summer for tans.

'I've brought you some sandwiches up from the delicatessen: pastrami on rye bread, is that OK?' Her voice has that soft husky quality that makes you think of melting honey and rustling leaves.

I nodded. I'd no idea what pastrami was. I didn't care. When the delivery girl looks and sounds like that, frog-spawn on toast would taste just fine.

She cleared a space on the desk, lowered the tray and the aroma of freshly ground coffee began to waft over. She wrapped a napkin around the handle of the pot, lifted it and began to pour. Her nails were the same vibrant red as her lips and skirt.

'I buzzed you about ten. You must have come in even later than usual.'

I swallowed a mouthful of pastrami on rye, and said, 'I had to visit a client.'

'You've got a client?' She injected a note of gentle irony into her voice.

I nodded. 'Building contractor. Lives in some fancy modern house near Saddleworth.'

14

She came round to my side of the desk, perched her neat little posterior on the battered wood, and crossed her legs. Close up, the sound of silk sliding over silk was like an electric shock.

She said, 'You mean that place called Ravenstone House?'

I only half-heard her. I was gazing at rounded knees and the sweep of thigh under taut, red cloth. Her stockings were black, her shoes flimsy and high-heeled. And then I realized she was waiting for an answer. I gazed up into her face, raised an eyebrow and looked vacant.

'Ravenstone House,' she repeated. 'Is that where you've been?' Her mouth pulled into that half-pleased, half-reproachful smile she always gives me when she knows I'm ogling her.

I nodded. 'That's the place. Rough-hewn stone, lots of glass, indoor pool not much bigger than Windermere.'

'They're always doing articles about it in the house-beautiful magazines,' she said. 'His wife, Moira . . . Mandy . . . '

'Mona,' I prompted.

'Sure, Mona. She used to be a fashion model. Quite famous: international.'

I swallowed another mouthful of pastrami on rye and said, 'I saw her. I'm not surprised.'

15

'Oh?' Melody's voice became a couple of degrees cooler, her eyes a little wary.

I guess she doesn't like me associating with women that look like Mona Saunders. In a pathetic, adolescent way, that never fails to please me.

'She was wearing a swimsuit. She'd just taken a dip in the pool,' I said.

'Really. That must have been thrilling for you.' Her voice was icy now. 'I suppose someone's been stealing her husband's sand.'

'Sorry?'

'Is that why they hired you, because someone's stealing sand from his builders' yard?'

I grinned up at her. 'No, it's something more personal than that.'

'You mean he's lost his hairpiece?'

'He's hired me to keep an eye on his wife. He thinks she might be cheating.'

She sniffed. 'You'll be seeing a good deal more of her, then.'

'I don't think I could see much more than I did this morning.'

'Oh, you never can tell,' she said brightly. 'Who knows what delights might be in store once you start pressing your blood-shot little eye to the keyhole?'

I drained the last of the coffee, let my grin widen. She glared down at me, blue eyes flashing, telling me how much she disapproved. Presently she slid from the desk, took the cup, then came very close as she reached over and picked up the tray. I caught her perfume: something sweet and flowery, the sort of thing a young girl might wear if she could afford it.

'Thanks for the sandwich and coffee.'

'Think nothing of it. I'm sure Mavis Saunders would have rustled you up something far more appetizing.'

'*Mona*,' I said. 'Not Mavis.'

She gave another disparaging little sniff, then turned and strutted out of the office, her high heels tap-tapping angrily all the way down to the carpeted landing on the floor below.

I got my feet up on the desk, closed my eyes, relaxed back in the swivel chair. The murmur of down-town traffic, the shuffle of pedestrians on the pavement below, seeped in through the open window. She must have moved like a cat on velvet. I didn't hear her come in; just sensed I was no longer alone. I raised an eyelid a millimetre, saw her standing in the middle of the room, perfectly erect, feet together, arms hanging straight down by her sides. She was wearing a short-sleeved white dress, white sandals and tiny white gloves that didn't cover her wrists. Her face was devoid of make-up and her huge dark eyes were holding me in an unblinking stare. It was as if a beautiful apparition had drifted in through the wall to haunt me.

I got my eyes open, swung my legs off the desk and sat up in the chair.

'So it is you,' she said. Triumph and reproach mingled in her refined voice.

'Won't you take a seat?' I nodded towards a fold of red plastic.

She sat on the edge of the chair, decorously, almost primly: legs pressed together, tiny white bag nestling on her lap, her back straight as the pathway to heaven.

'How can I help you, Mrs Saunders?'

She ignored my question; asked one instead. 'Why did my husband hire you, Mr Lomax?'

'What makes you so sure he's hired me?'

'Why else would someone like you visit the house?'

'Like he told you, I'm interested in holiday property: time-share flats.'

She didn't speak, just gazed at me.

Presently I said, 'How did you find me? I don't think your husband mentioned my name.'

'Cheque stub,' she said. 'He's very meticulous with business matters. He always records the payee's name. When I had that, I was able to get your address from the telephone directory.'

'And do you always suss out your husband's business associates?'

She smiled, not enough to reach her eyes, but enough to make the dimples show. 'Of course not. I just had a feeling about you. You seemed different somehow.'

I looked at her. Her face would have launched the American Seventh Fleet; her figure would have made the Russian Navy mutiny. Her big dark eyes looked right back, viewing me with something between distaste and curiosity.

She said, 'He's hired you to follow me, hasn't he?'

'Why would he do that?'

She shrugged. 'Oh, I don't know. He's been subdued recently, not himself. Something's worrying him badly, making him a little paranoid. He's suspicious and jealous of everyone. At first I found it flattering, but when it gets to be so obsessive it becomes mean and destructive. That's how it's been for quite a while. That's why I didn't need a computer to work out what you were doing at the house, once I'd discovered your name and what you do for a living.'

'Your husband didn't seem the neurotically jealous type to me, Mrs Saunders. More your outgoing, generous, fun-loving kind of guy.'

She gave me a tired little smile. 'You're describing him the way I remember him; the way he used to be when we were first married. He even suspects my hairdresser now, and if you knew my hairdresser you'd realize how ridiculous that is.'

I allowed my eyes to wander over her, from the dark almost black hair down to slender ankles and tiny white sandals. Her silky white dress was loose and flowing, her stockings sheer. She didn't have that scrawny anorexic look that fashion models seem to strive for. Maybe she'd put on a few pounds since she'd married. It suited her. It suited her just fine. A replay of Rex Saunders's warning began to whisper through my mind: 'Don't fall for her yourself, Lomax, and start shooting me a load of lies.' I took a couple of deep breaths, leant forward, linked my fingers on the blotter, tried to appear professional and detached.

'Well?' she said.

'Well, what?'

'Has he hired you to spy on me?'

'We're doing a little business together, Mrs Saunders, that's all.'

'And you're in the wrong business, Mr Lomax. The way you manage to keep on evading questions, you should be a politician. And I don't care what you say, I know he's hired you to watch me.'

She gave an exasperated little sigh, opened her bag, took out a diary and began to leaf through its tiny pages. 'I'll save you some time, Mr Lomax, and my husband some money. Seven-thirty tonight, I'm going to Saddleworth vicarage to play bridge. At one tomorrow, I'm lunching with the chairwoman of the Hospital Management Committee at Wetherton Country Club; at three, I'm going to the Vita Studio for a sauna and massage; I expect to be home by five and to have dinner ready by seven. Thursday, I'll be at home all day, but in the evening I'm opening a charity fashion show in the village hall. Friday, I . . . '

'How long have you been married, Mrs Saunders?' I asked her that to cut her short. She'd told me what a pillar of the community she was and her voice was becoming tearful, her Irish accent more noticeable.

'Ten years,' she said. 'I gave up everything to marry him. Successful career, my parents' happiness, practising my faith; he's divorced and I'm a Catholic. And it all seemed worth it, until last year. Then something began to worry him. Or someone else came along. Things haven't been right between us for months.'

'Someone else?'

'Some woman, Mr Lomax, or women;

21

there's maybe more than one. It's crazy, really; he's hired you to watch me, but it should be the other way round.'

I looked at her. It didn't bore me. In fact, I couldn't take my eyes off her. Looking at her was like being slammed by a lace pillow stuffed with warm, scented silk. I couldn't imagine her husband having a roving eye. But then, ten years is ten years, and jewellers grow accustomed to handling fine stones.

'I don't think we should be talking like this, Mrs Saunders. Like I said, I'm only doing a little business with your husband.'

'Don't patronize me. I know very well what he's hired you for.'

She dropped the diary back into her bag, clicked it shut, then rose to her feet and gazed down at me. I tried to make sense of the specks of light that were shining in those huge dark eyes.

'You know, Mr Lomax, you remind me a little of my husband; the way he was when we first met. He wasn't always paunchy and bald.'

She held out her hand. It was an instinctively regal gesture. I didn't know whether to kiss it or shake it. I stood up, reached over the desk, wrapped my paw around it and shook. I noticed she had pearl studs clipped to her ears. They matched the tiny pearls stitched to the bodice of her dress and handbag.

'Do you generally do this kind of work, Mr Lomax? Spy on errant wives, I mean.' I could hear the disappointment in her voice. I felt like a scruffy fourth-grade kid who's been caught picking his nose by the gorgeous young school-ma'am.

'Who said anything about spying on people?' I met her gaze for a moment, then added, 'I mostly stick to commercial work: fraud, insurance swindles, things like that.'

I let go of her hand. She turned and headed for the door. When she was about to step through into the waiting-room, she looked back and said, 'I'll see you tomorrow, Mr Lomax.'

'Tomorrow?'

She smiled. 'Slouched down in your car, outside the Wetherton Country Club.'

I smiled back.

'I'll have some sandwiches sent out. I wouldn't want you to starve while you're keeping your eye on me.'

★ ★ ★

I spent what was left of the afternoon drafting a report on a supermarket swindle: the manager and a couple of check-out girls had

23

got it together in more ways than one and profits were dwindling. When I was satisfied it wouldn't sound too bad read out in court, I decided to call it a day, clipped the papers together and headed for the ground floor, glad to be out of the fusty attic and down where it was cooler.

I wandered over to see Melody; found her sitting in an empty office, frowning into a computer screen. The day hadn't jaded her. She was still as crisp and fresh as a spring morning.

She glanced up. Her features began to soften into a smile, then suddenly became reproving. 'Mavis paid you a call, then?'

'Mona,' I corrected, then tried an appealing grin as I held up the swatch of papers.

'If you spent less time chatting up your clients' wives, you could do your own typing.'

'It was a heart-to-heart. Serious stuff. She's a very troubled woman.'

Melody leant back in her chair and pressed her fingertips together. 'Troubled? I thought she *was* the trouble.'

I smiled down at her.

'You're being paid to watch her, not give her a shoulder to cry on. Hubby could get upset.' She reached up to take the papers.

I held on and said, 'Maybe we could dine together tonight?'

Surprise must have chased away the spiteful little thoughts about Mona Saunders because she began to smile. 'Are you doing the cooking?'

I got rid of the silly grin and did my best to make my voice gentle as I said, 'That could damage something rare and tender; stop it growing into something beautiful.'

'Rare and tender!' She burst out laughing.

I let her tug the papers from my fingers. She tossed them into a tray, looked back up at me, and then the laughter erupted again. It was uncontrollable this time, husky and low, sexier than Eve in her fig-leaf.

'Are we talking steaks or relationships?' She was still giggling.

'You know darned well what I'm talking about. I thought we might motor into Ramford, have a meal at Luigi's.'

'It won't be like last time, will it?' Her tone was reproachful, but she was beginning to look interested.

'You'll never forgive me for that. Clients call and sometimes I can't say no. And I couldn't get you on your mobile.'

'Radar wouldn't have reached me in that cellar place. I waited more than an hour, Paul, drinking spritzers and looking stupid.'

Memories were making her indignant and she was frowning up at me. Suddenly her face

25

softened and she let out a husky little laugh. 'OK, Paul. Dinner at Luigi's would be very nice.'

'I'll book a table and pick you up at seven.' I heaved myself off the desk and headed out.

'Paul . . . '

I looked back at her across the empty desks.

'Just dinner. The evening ends after dinner. And we'll go Dutch.'

'So, it ends after dinner, but we're not going Dutch.'

3

Melody was ready. She must have been watching for me out of the bay window of her neat and not-so-small semi-detached. When I pulled up at the gate, she was closing the front door and turning the key in the lock. I figured it wasn't that she couldn't wait to see me: more a reluctance to have me invade the privacy of her home.

She stashed the keys in a black purse as she walked down the path. Her long cream topcoat was open, flashing me glimpses of a little black dress. I pushed open the door and soft fabric and fragrance flowed into the front of the car.

She gave me a demure little smile and said, 'You're on time: I can't believe it,' then drew the seatbelt over. When she turned to click the fastener home, her hair brushed my face. She'd washed it in something restrained and expensive; not the sort of thing you'd find the local rugger team using, even in Barfield. The dress was cut low at the top, and the hemline wandered the frontier between provocation and decorum. Provocation was winning on points and my pulse

27

was beating a little faster.

'Well . . . ?'

'Well, what?' I said gruffly.

'Take me to Ramford. I'm feeling peckish.'

'You're looking gorgeous . . . '

The demure little smile widened into something altogether more sexy. She kissed the tip of her finger and touched my cheek.

' . . . in fact, you're heart-stopping.'

'Heart-stopping!' She began to laugh. Demure had gone now. This was a throaty, happy, sexy sound. 'That's a new one. You can be awfully sweet when you're not making those facile remarks, Paul.'

I brushed a fall of hair from her cheek. She didn't seem to mind, so I just went on gazing at her.

'The car, Paul: put it in gear and let out the clutch. And don't forget, the evening begins and ends with dinner.'

I dragged my eyes back to the road. It was the hardest thing I'd done all day. Minutes later, we were cruising along country lanes.

'Shouldn't we be heading for the motor-way?'

'I've got to pay a call at Saddleworth vicarage.'

'We finally get to go out to dinner, and you decide to visit the vicar.'

'We're not going in. I just have to watch the

28

house for a few minutes.' I cruised up a steep rise to the church, then pulled off the narrow road and bumped over rough grass, keeping close to the graveyard wall. Leaves and branches rustled over the roof of the car as we moved under some trees; then we reached a corner and could see clear down into the gravel-covered yard of an old stone vicarage.

A couple of cars were already parked and a four-wheel-drive was just pulling in. I was beginning to wonder if I'd left it too late when a white Mercedes swung through the gateway.

I reached between the seats and grabbed the camera, just managed to switch it on and steady the telephoto lens against the dash when Mona climbed out and slammed the door.

Melody sniffed. 'Powder-blue twin set and pearls. And that old tweed skirt. She was trying a lot harder for you this afternoon.'

I squeezed the trigger: the camera began to take sequence shots as Mona crossed the gravel, heading for the open door of the vicarage. A tall, scrawny guy with a florid face and white hair stepped down from the big four-by-four and loped towards her. He looked to be about sixty. Maybe Mona was making *his* juices flow faster, but I guessed he wouldn't be doing much for her.

A short fussy-looking man in a dog collar appeared in the doorway. When he saw Mona, he threw his arms wide and through the telephoto lens I could see him mouthing, 'Mona, how lovely to see you.' She climbed the steps and when she went through the doorway, he wrapped his arm around her shoulders and led her inside. Maybe she made the vicar's juices flow faster, too.

'Is that it?' Melody sounded frosty. 'You don't seem to do very much for all the money you earn.'

'Saunders is wasting his money. I'm pretty sure she's not a cheater. He's not young any more; maybe he's starting to feel vulnerable instead of invincible and Mona's making him a little paranoid. Anyway, what I've just done isn't much use. I should be here when she comes out. See if she leaves with anyone; check where she goes.'

She sniffed disdainfully. 'Seems to me it's the kind of job pervy men would pay Saunders to let them do. And don't worry about me. Let's get some fish and chips and eat them out of the paper while you sit here and ogle her when she comes out.'

'Me, ogle?' Laughing softly, I slid the camera under the seat and reversed back on to the road, enjoying all over again that adolescent pleasure Melody's displeasure gives me.

'Yes, ogle! You even have to come here and get an eyeful when you're taking *me* out to dinner.'

Five minutes later we were dropping down on to the motorway and heading north for Ramford.

★   ★   ★

Luigi's deserved its reputation. Marble and mirrors, bright lights and big gilded chairs: it had plenty of glitter and class. The service from the dark-haired Italian waiters in their red waistcoats was as good as it gets these days. They certainly didn't mind a little flirty fetching and carrying for Melody, and the whole experience had put her in a bubbly mood.

I'll never know what made me do it. It couldn't have been the wine: I was driving, so Melody had drunk most of the bottle, plus a couple of brandies. And it wasn't just the way she looked that night, or the way she was making me feel. When I thought about it later, I wondered if Rex Saunders's questions had let the gremlins out of the bag: made me yearn for the things I'd lost.

Whatever it was, I was gazing at her across

a lorry-load of cream marble, she was taking delicate little sips at her coffee-cup and smiling right back at me, when I said, 'Marry me, Melody.' My voice was low and the happy chatter of the other diners was loud, but I could tell by the way her eyebrows jerked up that she'd heard me.

'Did you say what I think you said?' Her eyes were wide now.

'You heard it right.'

She began to laugh softly. 'I can't imagine what's got hold of you tonight, Paul.' When she put her cup down she was pressing her lips together to kill a smile, and when she spoke again the words were punctuated by helpless little giggles. 'It's not easy to talk in here. Let's split the bill and go.'

She didn't protest too much when I insisted on paying. A handsome young guy in the regulation red waistcoat brought her coat and I helped her into it, then we were heading out into the chilly darkness.

We had to walk a couple of blocks to the car. On the way, Melody talked about the meal, her business, my business; everything except the proposal. I sensed she was sticking to inconsequential chatter while she mulled over what I'd said. And I was beginning to realize I'd had a momentary lapse into insanity back there.

Locked inside the warmth of the car, heading back to Barfield, she fell silent for a while and her hand moved over mine. Presently she gave it a squeeze and said, 'I'm sorry, Paul.'

'Sorry?'

'Sorry for laughing like that. I don't know what came over me. I was so . . . shocked.' She giggled.

I knew that if I said a word she'd burst out laughing all over again. She gave my hand another little squeeze, then took hers away.

'It wouldn't work, Paul. You and me. It's crazy.'

'What's crazy about it? And what's so damn funny?' I muttered huffily.

She was really trying to hold back the laughter now. 'Of course it's not funny. I don't think it's . . . '

'Then why are you laughing fit to bust?'

'I . . . It was the shock. Oh, God, what can I say?'

'Saying what you feel might be a good idea.'

'I'm not marriage-minded, Paul. And I don't want a relationship. I'm comfortable as I am. Things are OK. The business is doing well; the house is paid for. I lead a quiet, ordered life. I like things the way they are, Paul. I don't want them changed.'

'It's me, isn't it? I'm not the kind of guy . . . '

'Don't be silly. It's got nothing to do with you.'

We rode on in silence. Rain began to spot the windscreen and I flicked on the wipers. And then the tyres started to hiss through the wet as it got heavier. I risked a glance at her. She wasn't laughing any more, so I said, 'How about someone to grow old and grey with? Don't you want that?'

She gave a little snort. 'If you don't change your job, you won't grow old and grey. And it doesn't work. The woman usually ends up on her own. When you need the love and companionship most, it's taken from you.'

She gazed out at the rain and the night for a few more wiper sweeps, and then her voice was almost inaudible as she said, 'Anyway, I tried that.'

'You've been married?'

'You see, you don't know the first thing about me,' she said reprovingly. 'I was twenty-two. Don't ask me how long ago that was. The honeymoon was a disappointment and it went downhill after that. Six months on, I found him in bed with some pubescent schoolgirl. If she'd been a week younger he'd have been jailed for it. The marriage lasted ten days short of a year. I don't intend to go down that road again.'

'It's not always like that.'

'Men's brains are in their groins, Paul, and that's putting it politely. It's the way they're programmed.'

'You're saying you couldn't trust me, is that it?'

She gave me a sideways glance. 'I'd trust you more than most, but you're exposed to all kinds of women.'

'So are other guys. What about doctors?'

'They take the Hippocratic oath, and they get struck off if they start any funny business. The Keyhole-Peepers' Club would probably give you the gold medal for endeavour if you started some serious hanky-panky.'

'I'd better renew my subscription.'

'Anyway, most men don't get involved with the kind of women you rub shoulders with. And these women always come with the work you say you don't want. I don't have to be very bright to work out why you take those cases, Paul.'

'There *are* good marriages,' I protested, gently. 'I had one.'

'And you'd bring the baggage of it with you. I could cope with the Rachel Palmers and little Miss What's Her Name, that cute red-head . . . '

'Bergman,' I prompted. 'Estelle Bergman.'

'Unforgettable, was she? I could even cope with fashion model Mona, but how would I compete with a dead woman? You've never stopped thinking about your wife, and you're still yearning for your little girl.'

That chilled me. What Saunders had started, she'd finished. I'd be weeks getting the dirty little gremlins back in the bag now. The weak and tender sex: all feelings and emotions. Deep down they've got iron-hard hearts. She must have known what that little bit of plain talking would do to me.

We were cruising through one of Barfield's more exclusive suburbs, closing in on Melody's home. I swung the Jag off the main estate road, drove more slowly past pleasant, well-maintained houses until I found her gate.

'Let me make you some coffee.'

'I thought it had to begin and end with dinner.'

'It can't end like this. Come in for some coffee.' She climbed out of the car, slammed the door and headed on up the path.

I felt demeaned. We'd known one another a long time. She didn't have to laugh herself sick at my proposal, then tear the plaster off festering wounds that still refused to heal. She could have let me down gently; said she was flattered but spoken for, that she was glad but gay, that she'd think about it and tell me later.

The engine was idling. I watched her fiddling with the key, then the front door opened and a light went on inside. I slid the car into gear and began to let out the clutch. Then I got to thinking I'd been stupid asking her in the first place, that I should try and be rational, not start acting like a drag queen with a migraine. So I switched off the ignition and followed her up the path.

She was looking into the hall mirror, pretending to tweak the odd strand of hair back into place. I stood close behind her and we gazed, tight-lipped, at our reflections for a while.

I helped her out of her coat and hooked it over a peg by the mirror. She didn't move away, so I slid my hands around her waist, palms resting on the swell of her hips, and began to kiss the side of her neck through her hair. She leant back into me, pressing hard enough to break a rib.

My thumbs were gently caressing the small of her back. She put her hands over mine and squeezed hard, making me wonder whether she was stopping them wandering or just telling me to go on. Her hair was all over my face and the rhythm of her breathing had suddenly changed: become slower and deeper.

'I'm sorry, Paul,' she whispered, then moaned a little while I went on caressing the small of her back and kissing her shoulders. I glanced at her reflection. Her eyes were tight shut, her lips parted, her mascara smudged a little.

She suddenly turned and faced me, slid her arms around my neck and hung on. 'I'm such a bitch. I shouldn't have said those things to you. But you scared me. I didn't know you felt that way, and I couldn't let you get the wrong idea. I'm not into marriage, Paul. I don't want to play mummies and daddies. I . . . ' The words had come out in a rush and her mouth was trembling now.

I leant forward and kissed her. It was very gentle, no more than a brushing of her lips. She let out another little moan and began to kiss me back; hard, hot, and open-mouthed. Her fingers were tangled in the hair at the back of my neck and she was pulling me close.

I felt a rapid little trembling against my chest, and with it a rush of pride at being able to excite her so much. And then I caught the atonal *cheep, cheep, cheep*. Squeezing against the more dramatic parts of Melody's anatomy had switched my mobile on.

She broke free and turned to face the

mirror again, making tut-tutting sounds at her reflection. I got the phone out, keyed it, and muttered my name and number.

'Where the hell have you been? I've been trying to get you for an hour.' The hoarse spieler's voice and the Yorkshire accent were unmistakable. 'I'd like you to come over, I've got to talk to you.'

'You mean right now?' I peered at my watch. It was a little after midnight.

'Yeah, right now.'

'Can't it wait until morning?'

'Tomorrow morning could be too late. Mona's gone missing. She went out at seven to the bridge club at the vicarage. She's usually back by ten, but there's no sign of her. I phoned the vicar and he said she left at the usual time. I'm worried. I'm as worried as hell.'

'There'll be a simple explanation. There almost always is. Perhaps she's . . . '

'Yeah, perhaps she's letting some evil little turd give her one.'

'How can my coming over now help? Maybe her car's broken down. Maybe you should phone the police.'

'She'd phone me if she had car problems, and I can't phone the police. Anyway, why should I when I've hired you?'

'Because there's more of them and they've

got bigger resources. Anyway, it's what you pay taxes for.'

'I can't call the police. Come over now and I'll explain. I didn't tell you everything this morning. Didn't think it mattered. Trouble is, I've upset some individuals who really don't care what they do or who they do it to. There's a chance they've got hold of Mona to get at me.'

'Sounds as though you really do need the police.'

'Can't. I've told you, I can't. I had a phone call a few minutes ago. A guy's coming over to see me. Said it was very personal, but he wouldn't tell me any more. I want you on the premises when he arrives. When he's said what he's got to say, we can decide whether you're handling it or whether we're calling the cops in. Or maybe we can laugh over a brandy if he just wants to talk to me about sod-all.'

'Why not call the cops in now?'

'I keep telling you, I *can't*. Don't make me beg, Lomax. They might have got Mona. And they're such sick bastards I'd rather she was in the sack with some other guy than with them. I'm scared. And you don't know how much it takes to make me admit that. I want you here. I want you here *now*.' The voice coming down the line was ragged with worry.

'OK,' I sighed. 'I'll come over. Fifteen minutes.' I slid the mobile inside my jacket.

Melody turned and faced me. I began to say sorry, but she just smiled at me and said, 'Thank him for me, will you?'

I raised an eyebrow.

'For throwing the bucket of cold water over us. Heaven knows where we'd have ended up if he'd not called.'

She stood on tiptoe and gave me a chaste little kiss, the sort of thing you might get from a maiden aunt. Then she pulled the door open and said, 'I'll see you tomorrow, Paul.'

Her tone was brisk and matter-of-fact. Heading off into the darkness, I began to wonder if the evening had ever happened.

4

Ravenstone House was a black silhouette against a night sky stained orange by the sodium glow of nearby Barfield. I swung the car off the narrow lane and motored on down a brick-paved driveway. Headlamp beams wavered over rough-hewn stone, probing windows as obscure as dark glasses on a blind man. I parked by the front door, killed the motor and climbed out. Away from the town, the air was colder and cleaner. I dragged in a couple of lungfuls then pressed the bell button. I heard distant chimes, waited, no one came.

The door was a lot of narrow vertical strips of coloured glass set between strips of polished wood. I got my eye up close. A faint diffused glow seemed to be coming from deep within. I pounded the door, shattering the stillness of the house and the night. All it got me was skinned knuckles and some faint echoes.

I tried the door. It was locked. I started to walk around the house, hoping I'd complete the round trip before dawn. Trudging over more of the fancy brick paving, I peered in dark windows: some were curtained, through others I could make out the dim shapes of furniture within.

I reached a corner, then headed down the windowless north-facing side of the house. The blocks of rough-hewn stone were massive here, and a screen of cypress trees crowded in on the narrow path. I turned into a small yard enclosed on three sides by the walls of the house. Light was leaking out from between the slats of a Venetian blind that closed off the smallest window I'd seen so far. There was a door alongside.

I skipped the knock-knock routine and worked the handle. It opened. I stepped inside, on to big yellow terrazzo tiles. The bright fluorescent lights were painful after the dark and made me blink as I took in the scene. Deep porcelain sinks, panelled cupboard doors, food mixers, Aga cooker, marbled worktops, copper pans: the kind of classy paraphernalia that had earned the Saunders' residence a mention in most of the glossy magazines. It looked clean and neat and as sterile as an operating theatre.

I crossed over the tiles to a door in the far wall, pulled it open and yelled, 'Anybody home?' into the darkness. There was no answer.

I stood there for a few moments, trying to

get my bearings. I gave up. The house seemed to be laid out in an open, rambling way where one huge room gave on to another. My eyes were adjusting to the gloom again. I made out an oval dining-table and chairs and, beyond the pool of light from the kitchen door, a couple of leather chesterfields.

An uneasy feeling was stirring inside me. I held my breath and listened to the silence pervading that sprawling collection of dark, deserted rooms. The house wasn't whispering any secrets to me. I closed the door, retraced my steps across the kitchen, and went out into the night.

I left the enclosed yard and continued the circuit of the house. It had been designed to face south, trap the sun and retain its heat. I guessed I was walking along the blind back wall of the swimming-pool. I turned a corner, ploughed my way through shrubs and bushes, then turned another and saw the glazed south wall of the pool stretching out in front of me.

Lights gleamed at the far end where I'd sat with Rex Saunders that morning. I tried to take a peek inside, but the huge panes of glass were misty with condensation. Close by me was the door he'd used to let me out. I pressed the handle and when I shoved it, it squealed open. Maybe he'd forgotten to lock it.

I threaded my way between the big stone troughs crammed with ferns and miniature palms, heading towards the lights at the house end of the pool. I rounded a clump of foliage arranged along a sweeping projection that almost divided the expanse of water. I saw him then, floating on his back: gaudy cotton shorts, white torso, weather beaten arms and face.

When I closed in, I could make out the shocked staring eyes and the gaping mouth. It was Saunders all right, and I knew I could skip the kiss-of-life routine. The lower half of his chest was a pulpy mess of skin, fat and bloody tissue. It looked like a shotgun job: large bore, close range.

A smell of cordite lingered in the air, not quite masked by the pungent aroma of chlorine. He'd stopped bleeding. The crimson cloud had detached itself from his body and was being sucked, wraith-like, into a grille let into the side of the pool. Mona wouldn't make him jealous any more. He was moving on, like the blood slowly drifting down to the filters beneath the pool.

One of the canvas chairs we'd sat on that morning was over-turned. Papers had spilled out of a folder and were scattered over the table and floor. I saw the big blue chequebook down beside a stone plant trough, stepped over and picked it up. I flicked through, saw my name, that day's date and a cash amount entered on one of the stubs. I slid the book into my pocket. It was an instinctive act of self-preservation.

I thought of Mona Saunders. My nerve endings were screaming at me to clear out fast, but I wiped the sweat from the palms of my hands and began to make a quick search of the place. I didn't have a torch, so I flicked on lights as I went, working switches and door handles through a handkerchief.

I felt like a stagehand lighting up a set. There was no paint or plaster, just rough stone, dark polished wood, glass and exposed beams. Heavy blue drapes on wooden rods and a scattering of fine oriental rugs softened the effect a little. Unframed oil paintings, mostly massive abstract daubs, covered up two or three acres of stone and stopped it from getting too boring.

The lounge, with its massive island fireplace, rose through two storeys, clear up to the boarded underside of the sloping roof. A spiral staircase gave access to a gallery that ran the width of the room. Doors were ranged along the gallery, so I climbed up, worked my way through four expensively austere bedrooms, then headed along a short passage and found myself looking down into

46

the entrance hall. I paused there for a while. The huge rambling place was more a rough-hewn enclosure of space than a house. It was dead and silent, like a department store on Christmas Day.

I checked a bathroom that had a his and hers of almost everything: I guess the family that sprays together doesn't always stay together. Then I moved on down another short passage, found the master bedroom with a bathroom and dressing-room *en suite* and ivory-coloured carpet wall-to-wall. Mona must have felt the need for something to wriggle her toes in. The four poster bed had a deep carved headboard, Spanish style, but no canopy. A cream silk coverlet had been folded down to expose silk pillows. No one had slept there that night; no one had slept in any of the other bedrooms, either. A lacy white négligé was draped over the back of a chair. The room was warm and dry and faintly perfumed.

When I killed the light I could see through a big picture window, clear over the crest of a tree-covered rise. Barfield sprawled like a jewelled harlot in the valley beyond; scintillating, spilling out a million watts of wasted light.

I headed down to the ground floor by way of a more or less conventional flight of stairs that ended in a passage near the swimming-pool. I'd checked all the rooms and some walk-in cupboards, and wiped my prints off the kitchen doors. Mona Saunders wasn't at home.

I went back to the pool. The red stain had been sucked away, and the water was sparkling and clear again. Rex Saunders had drifted closer to the side. I looked down into his wide shocked eyes for a moment, then continued on around the plant troughs.

I left by the door at the far end of the pool, wiped off the handles, dragged it shut, then made my way round to the front of the house and climbed into the car. I didn't switch on the lights until I reached the main Barfield Road. It didn't matter: I didn't see cars or people until I was almost back in town.

I pulled into a lay-by just beyond a bridge, changed into some wellingtons I keep in the boot, then dropped my down-at-heel brogues into the canal. I'd left my muddy footprints all over the Saunders' place, stamped my seal of approval on to most of the rugs and carpets. Forensics could probably paint an identikit picture from a footprint in a rug these days.

★　★　★

They didn't bother to knock. They didn't show me their identity cards, either. They didn't have to. 'Crime Squad' was written into every crease of their crumpled suits and the quiet way they moved into the office and filled it with an arrogant brutish presence. The church clock across the street had just chimed three. I'd expected them earlier; at least six hours earlier.

'Lomax?' The older one asked that.

I nodded, studied the grey eyes, florid features and tobacco-coloured hair that was streaked with grey.

The men dragged red plastic chairs up close to the desk and flopped down.

'I'm Sloane, he's Mace, Barfield CID.' The inflections in his throaty voice told me he'd been born close by and hadn't forgotten it.

I tried to look relaxed.

They eyed me across the clutter on the desk. The one called Mace looked pasty and bloodless, with dark jowls that would need shaving twice a day. His black hair was cut short and lightly oiled. They both had the humourless, tight-lipped mouths and cold eyes of men who trade in the currency of humanity's shabby lies.

'You're a private investigator?' Sloane asked.

I nodded, kept up the genial smile.

'Make much?' Mace stretched out, settled down in the chair, his feet invading the knee hole of the desk. He took a match from his pocket and sharpened it by splitting the end.

'I do OK,' I said, then watched him gazing contemptuously around the room while he probed the spaces between his teeth.

Sloane said, 'Do you know a bloke called Saunders? Rex Saunders?'

'You mean the one that lives at Ravenstone House?'

He nodded.

I told them I did.

'Client of yours, is he?' Mace was a Londoner, a Cockney.

'We're doing a little business together.' I remembered to stick to the present tense; the murder hadn't been reported yet.

'What's that supposed to mean?' Sloane grated. Mace went on probing his teeth.

'It means he's a business acquaintance of mine.'

'You've got him on the books?' Mace spat crud and fragments of matchstick towards the carpet, then began to give his nails a manicure. The backs of his fingers were darkened by tufts of bristly black hair.

I shook my head. The denial was true as far as it went; I didn't keep any books.

'You're a taciturn sod, Lomax.' Sloane's

voice was humourless when he said that.

'What was your business with him, then, if he wasn't on your books?' Mace asked.

'Flats. Time-share flats. Marbella.'

They looked at one another. Sloane wasn't bothering to hide the grin.

Mace frowned, looked thoughtful, said, 'Marbella: that's a place just south of Cleethorpes, isn't it?'

They both grinned at me.

'Spain,' Sloane said. 'Marbella's in Spain. It's Mablethorpe that's near Cleethorpes.'

'Yeah, that's it: Mablethorpe.' Mace wiped the matchstick on his sleeve and gazed around the office. 'Maybe you timeshare this dump, Lomax,' he sneered.

I looked at him, said nothing.

Sloane said, 'Saunders's wife. Do you know her, Lomax?'

'I've seen her at the house. I couldn't say I know her.'

'You got lucky. She said your business was time-share flats, too.'

I shrugged, said, 'And what does Mr Saunders say?'

'He's not saying anything.'

I gazed from one pair of watchful calculating eyes to the other. Mace looked down, got to work on the nails of his other bristle-backed hand.

'When did you last see Rex Saunders?' Sloane asked.

'Yesterday morning. At Ravenstone House.'

Sloane looked at Mace and I thought he inclined his head towards the door. It was a barely noticeable movement.

Mace said, 'Where's the khazi?' in his Cockney voice.

'Small door, top of the landing.'

He tucked the remains of the matchstick into his breast-pocket, stood up and headed on out. I was relieved he felt the need to relieve himself, even if he was only pretending. Another minute and he'd have slipped his shoes and socks off, got a foot up on the desk and started giving himself a pedicure.

When doors had finished slamming, Sloane rose slowly, leant over the desk and shoved his face close to mine. 'Don't mess me about, Lomax. You're no more interested in time-share flats than I am. What did Saunders hire you for?'

I could smell cigarette smoke on his breath. The bridge of his nose and his cheeks were marked with a tracery of fine red veins. His grey eyes were bloodshot. I figured he was two, maybe three, haircuts and a shave away from retirement.

'We're trying to do a deal on a flat. Ask Saunders, he'll tell you the same,' I said.

'Saunders won't be doing deals any more, Lomax. He's handed in his dinner bowl.'

I jacked my eyebrows up. 'He looked fine yesterday.'

Sloane scowled, reached across the desk and grabbed me by the lapels. 'I know a lot about you, Lomax. You're wifeless, motherless, friendless and skint. I can take you inside, keep you there a while, maybe even put you out of business, and no one's going to say a dicky-bird. So don't fool me around. Tell me what Saunders wanted you for.'

'Like I already told you, like his wife told you: time-share flats.'

He heaved me back in the chair and flopped down in his own. I heard clanking noises, the sound of a toilet flush, then the Cockney called Mace wandered back into the room.

'You've got a museumpiece there, Lomax.' He sat down, looked at Sloane, and said, 'It's all crammed into a ruddy cupboard, Chief. A khazi in a cupboard.' He laughed happily. Sloane didn't even smile.

We stared at one another across the desk. Big, brutish, arrogant; and their cold eyes were alert and watchful. I couldn't imagine these men helping old ladies across the street, and kids would be too scared to ask the time.

Presently Sloane said, 'How tall are you, Lomax?'

'Six-one.'

He eyed me shrewdly. 'You're a hard, muscular kind of guy, just starting to get a little meaty. I'd say you weigh around one-ninety, two hundred pounds.'

'You're probably right.'

'And I bet you take a size nine.'

'Yeah, size nine. You should run a booth on a fairground.'

'Forensic report says some fourteen-stone bloke wearing size nines with a hole in the right sole tramped all over the Saunders' place. Every door he went through's been wiped clean.'

'No!'

'Yeah.'

'Do I look as though I'd wear shoes with worn-through soles?'

'You look as though you'd go around barefoot,' Sloane muttered.

Mace said, 'Just lift your plates of meat on to the desk, Lomax.'

I rolled the chair back, swung my feet up. 'Maybe you'd like to check through the collection at home?'

'We already have,' Sloane said.

'And *now* you're going to show me the warrant.'

Sloane groped inside his jacket, pulled out a paper, unfolded it, and laid it on the desk. I couldn't make out the justice's signature, but it was a warrant to search all right. I handed it back. Sloane pocketed it.

'We left it like we found it,' Mace said. 'Looking like an explosion in an Oxfam shop.'

'Thanks,' I said. 'I wouldn't want my valet to get any funny ideas.'

They stood up. Sloane said, 'We'll be in touch, Lomax.'

I heard the patter of footsteps out in the waiting-room, and Mace and Sloane turned to get a better view as Melody swirled into the office, carrying the afternoon tray.

She stopped short when she saw I had company, said, 'Sorry, Paul, I didn't realize these gentlemen were with you.'

'It's OK, they're just leaving.' I glanced up at their faces. Mace was leering and there was even a glitter in Sloane's bloodshot little eyes.

Melody gave Mace a frosty look. Maybe she got all the ogling she needed from me. Blonde hair had been gathered up on her head, exposing red ear-studs that matched the red silk dress. When her baby-blues glanced at Sloane, her glossy red lips seemed to tighten with an instinctive disapproval.

'This is Inspector Mace and Inspector Sloane, Barfield CID.,' I said.

'Chief Inspector,' Sloane corrected.

Melody smiled sweetly. 'He's not been gatecrashing Ann Summers parties again, has he?'

Mace sniggered. Sloane coughed, dragged his eyes off the size fourteen shape poured into the size twelve dress and looked at me. 'Like I said, we'll be in touch, Lomax. But if you've got anything to tell us, just give me a ring.' They turned and headed on out.

I called after them, 'Hey, what did he die of?'

Sloane put his head round the door and looked back at me. 'Don't fool around, Lomax. You already know what he died of.'

5

I decided to give the commuter tailbacks a miss that evening; wait in the office until the nightly convoys had wound their way out of town. An overcast sky was making it darker than it should have been and a gusting wind was rattling the window, driving rain against the glass. I dragged open the bottom drawer of the desk, took out a bottle, poured a few fingers of Scotch into the cup I'd drunk tea from a couple of hours earlier, and began to nuzzle it.

I pulled Rex Saunders's cheque from my pocket, ran my eyes longingly over the figures, then burnt it in the waste bin: I might have known I'd never make money that easy. I remembered the chequebook I'd taken from the poolside, groped in my jacket, found it, and flicked through the stubs. Mona Saunders had been right. Her husband had been methodical when it came to money matters: each stub was made out with the payment details. It looked like a personal chequebook. There didn't seem to be any items connected with his building business. The dates ranged over the past six months and there were only two cheques left in the book.

I was just going to incinerate it in the bin when I heard a knocking on the outer door, faint and timid. I waited, listened to the gusting wind and the rain peppering the window, then heard it again, a little louder this time. I slid the chequebook under the blotter, went over to the door and peered through the gloomy waiting-room.

He jumped when he saw me. 'Mr Lomax, Mr Paul Lomax?' His startled voice was higher than tenor, not quite contralto.

'Yeah, that's me.'

'May I talk with you for a few moments?'

'Sure, why not? Come on through.'

I flicked the lights on, pulled the blind down, got back behind the desk.

Black fashion boots with pointed toes and raised heels made him about five-nine tall. He was thin, almost emaciated. Shiny black leather pants hugged his scrawny calves and thighs. A black leather bomber jacket was unzipped to show off a shocking-pink silk shirt. The shirt was partly unbuttoned. I could see a wedge of tanned chest and two or three medallions. He was like a coiled spring, twanging with nervous energy.

'Sit down, Mr . . . ?'

'Vivian. Vivian Delmar.'

He sat down; spindly legs tucked under the

chair, hands grasping bony knees. Rings were crammed on to long, thin fingers; a chunky gold bracelet was wrapped around a slender wrist.

'How can I help you, Mr Delmar?'

'Mona Saunders asked me to come and see you. And it's Vivian. Do call me Vivian,' he gushed. Brown eyes that were moist and soft flickered over me nervously. He had a deep sallow tan, the kind of thing you get lying under a lamp, and the skin of his face was tight-stretched over small, angular features. Drops of rain glistened on the black curls that were massed around his head.

'You're a friend of Mrs Saunders?' I asked.

'Yes, I suppose you could say we've become friends. I'm Mona's hairdresser. Salon Delmar. It's unisex. Do you know it?'

I shook my head. My barber thought he was innovating when he did short back and sides. I studied him some more. When he talked, his mouth was very mobile, his whole face radiant with an eagerness to please. A fragrance was filling the office. It was sweet and cloying. I guessed it was the stuff he used for setting women's hair; either that, or the aftershave he drenched himself in cost less than five pence a quart.

'Why did she want you to contact me?' I said.

He leant forward and his voice dropped to a whisper. 'Her husband was killed last night.'

'Killed?'

'The police told her it was a shotgun.' He gave a little gasp. 'Such a shock for the poor love. And now she thinks she's being watched by the police, and her husband's business associates are being utterly beastly to her.'

'Where do I fit into all this?'

'She needs help, Mr Lomax, but she daren't come and see you herself. In fact, she's got the jitters so bad she thinks the phone's being tapped and she wouldn't even ring you.'

'Is she still at Ravenstone House?'

He pouted and shook the mass of tight black curls. 'Heavens, no. She was too upset and scared to stay on in that big rambling place on her own. She's borrowed a friend's flat.' He mentioned a town-centre address, then asked, 'Do you think the police could be watching her, Mr Lomax?'

I shrugged. 'It's possible. After all, they are doing a murder investigation.'

He grimaced at that, then said, 'Stupid brutes. She wouldn't hurt a fly.' Big brown eyes gave me the once-over, and his voice became coaxing. 'She'd like to talk to you. Tonight, if you can manage it.'

I thought about that one. I hadn't wanted

the job her husband had bribed me into taking. I wanted to get involved with the mess Mona was in even less.

He must have noticed some hardening of my expression, sensed I was going to refuse, because he made his near contralto voice urgent and said, 'She's frightened, Mr Lomax. Absolutely terrified. At least come and see her.'

'How do you know all this?'

'She came to the salon, late this afternoon. White as a sheet, she was, the poor love. I got one of the girls to make her a cup of tea. She told me what had happened; asked me if I'd bring a message to you. She was afraid that if she came herself, the police would follow her and you might not be able to help.'

'Why should she be worried about the police, Mr Delmar?'

'All I know is, she's scared to death, Mr Lomax, and she's asking for your help. And do call me Vivian,' he insisted petulantly.

I conjured up a mental picture of Mona Saunders: the long dark hair, the sensational figure; classy, glamorous, too beautiful to be true. The vision was drowning out the inner voices that were clamouring at me, telling me to give Mona's problems a miss.

Eventually I sighed and said, 'OK, I'll meet

61

her around eight. Did she have anywhere in mind?'

He was beaming at me now. 'I've got a flat over the shopping precinct, near the place where Mona's staying. She can reach it by walking round the upper access deck. I thought that if you arrived before she did, then gave her a few minutes to get clear before you left, anyone following her wouldn't realize you'd met.'

I grinned across the desk at him. He'd worked out all the moves. Maybe he should join what Melody called the Keyhole-Peepers' Club, too. I took down the address he gave me. It all sounded a little paranoid, but it wouldn't do any harm to go along with the idea.

'I'll be there at eight then, Mr Del . . . Vivian.'

He beamed some more, jack-knifed to his feet and came up to the desk. 'Thanks, Mr Lomax. She'll be so relieved when I tell her, the poor love.' He held out a hand. I grabbed it. It was like taking hold of a fistful of frankfurter sausages that had been dropped into a bag of tap washers. I saw him wince a little, then we exchanged goodbyes and I let go. He turned and strutted out, his principal boy's backside writhing around inside the leather pants like a python in a plastic sack.

I headed up to the main shopping mall. Rain glistened on brick walls and its pattering distorted the reflections of shop-window lights in the puddles.

The narrow opening was sandwiched between a pizza parlour and a chemist's, just as Delmar had described. I turned into it, trudged down a passage and emerged into a dimly lit parking area at the rear. I heard a scuffling sound: one of Barfield's ageing underachievers was stumbling around amongst waste bins in a compound behind the shops. I squeezed between a couple of cars, then climbed some concrete stairs to the access deck, striding on past doors and curtained windows. I found the number Delmar had given me and punched the bell. Musical chimes serenaded me while the rain seeped through my coat.

The door opened a few inches. I could see black curls and a big brown eye behind the taught links of a chain.

'Mr Delmar?'

'Oh, it's you, Mr Lomax.' He was breathless with relief.

The chain rattled; the door opened wide. As he waved me in he reminded me, all over again, to call him Vivian. He was wearing a

63

black velvet jacket, black bow-tie, and a shirt with frills up the front. His black pants weren't as tight as the leather items he'd worn earlier, and the patent-leather shoes made him look an inch shorter.

'I'm so pleased you've arrived,' he gushed. 'I'm taking the girls and boys from the salon out for a meal. My treat. We do it every month. I've got to collect some of the girls and I must fly, so come on through.'

He led me down a narrow hallway, through a door into a small sitting-room where the deep-pink carpet was springy and new-looking. A paler pink sofa and a couple of armchairs were arranged around a fancy electric fire in an Adam-style surround that had a marble hearth. There were plenty of lamps with gold and black shades, all set on low tables. The white walls were studded with bright little oil paintings that had a lot of gilded frame and not much canvas. Every flat surface was crowded with statuettes, paper-weights, enamelled boxes and similar bric-à-brac masquerading as *objets d'art*.

'Let me take your coat.'

I slipped it off and handed it to him.

'Gosh, it's huge, and the rain's made it so heavy. I'll hang it over a chair in the kitchen and put it near a radiator. Do sit down.'

He strutted off. I heard a chair being

dragged across a tiled floor, and then he hurried back.

'Can I get you a drink?'

'A whisky would be fine,' I said.

He went over to a silver drinks tray, unstoppered a heavy decanter and poured a generous shot into a cut-glass tumbler. He brought it over. I thanked him and he switched on the electric fire.

'I'll just give the central heating a top-up. Mona's going to be chilled through when she gets here.'

He disappeared for a few seconds. When he returned, there was an expensive-looking black overcoat with velvet lapel trimmings draped over his shoulders like a cloak. 'Mona shouldn't be long. Give her a drink for me. And don't forget to hook the security-chain on the door. I had it fitted because rowdies find their way up from the shops.' He looked me over, then added, 'But I don't suppose you'd need a safety-chain on *your* door.'

I sipped the spirit, grinned at him and said, 'Sometimes we all need a safety chain, Vivian.'

He beamed back at me, then left the room. Seconds later the outer door slammed and he was gone. I relaxed back on to the pink damask, sipped my Scotch and waited for Mona.

6

I didn't have to wait long, no more than a finger of Scotch, before the chimes were ding-donging down the hall. I put my glass on the marble hearth and went to open the door.

Mona Saunders got inside fast. I helped her out of her coat and hung it near the door, then watched slender fingers pluck at a knot and flick away the green silk scarf that was covering her hair. When she walked in front of me into the sitting-room, I got a feeling that the place was very familiar to her.

'Vivian Delmar asked me to give you a drink. What'll it be?' I asked.

'Brandy,' she said, and shivered.

'Anything with it?' I turned and looked back at her. She was sitting on the edge of an armchair, holding her hands towards the fire.

'No, just as it is.'

I poured her plenty, carried it over, then sat on the sofa facing her. She nuzzled the spirit and looked at me over the rim of her glass with those huge dark eyes. Her almost black hair had been swept back and secured with a couple of combs. I guessed she'd arranged it that way herself. It didn't look contrived enough to be Vivian's handiwork. She was doing more for a black woollen sweater than Montgolfier ever did for balloons. Her pleated skirt was made of some thick grey material and her shoes were meant for walking along wet pavements, not prancing around in a ballroom. I looked into her eyes, sipped my drink, said nothing.

'It was good of you to agree to come,' she said.

I raised an eyebrow.

'And very kind of Vivian to bring you the message. He's very sweet, but perhaps you realize now how silly my husband was to be suspicious of him.'

'Your husband didn't mention Vivian Delmar to me.'

'But he did hire you because he thought I was having an affair with someone, didn't he?'

The guy was dead. There was no point keeping this particular secret any more, so I said, 'Yes, Mrs Saunders, he did hire me to follow you, to give him reports on where you'd been and who with.'

'Do you often get involved in that kind of thing?'

'Hardly ever.'

'Then why do it for my husband?'

'He was paying me very well, Mrs Saunders. You could say he bribed me into taking the job.' I swallowed a mouthful of Scotch. She gazed at me with her big, mournful, new-widow's eyes. I wondered if she could tell I hadn't liked admitting I'd been bought.

'I want you to do a job for me, Mr Lomax.' She finished her drink, held out her glass, gave me a tight-lipped weepy kind of smile and said, 'Get me another, will you? Vivian won't mind.'

I gazed at her for a moment, then reached over and took her glass. I could hear the crack of the whip. It was faint, very faint, but it was there all right. With her looks and poise she'd maybe grown accustomed to men fawning around her all the time, and come to expect it. Or maybe she was letting me know I was just going to be the hired hand.

I lingered over the remains of my drink, then got up, went over to the tray and brought back a couple of refills.

She took her glass, then looked up at me as she asked, 'What was my husband paying you, Mr Lomax?'

I mentioned the figure. She sipped her drink, then said softly, 'I'll pay you the same if you'll help me: double, if you manage to clear up some problems for me.'

I let myself sink back into the sofa. 'Hadn't you better tell me what these problems are, Mrs Saunders? Then I'll decide whether or not I'm going to help you.' I didn't even try to keep the weariness out of my voice.

'I suppose Vivian told you Rex has been murdered.' Her face broke up when she said that. She looked away, sniffed, and swallowed a little, trying to get herself under control.

'Yeah,' I said softly. 'Vivian told me.'

'I think the police suspect me. At the very least they think it was because of me.' She gave me a wide-eyed look, then said, '*Me!*' in an indignant voice. Maybe she was telling me to sit up and take more notice.

'What makes you think they suspect you? Shock could be making you oversensitive.'

She looked down at her glass and shook her head. 'I kept things from them, Mr Lomax, and I think they know I did.'

I raised an eyebrow.

'I told them I came downstairs and found him dead in the pool.' She shivered, despite the heat glowing out of the three-bar fire. 'That's true, as far as it goes. I told them I didn't hear the sound of a gun, so they know I couldn't have been in the house when Rex was killed, but I didn't tell them I'd been out until the early hours.'

'And what time did you get in?'

'It was after one. I went upstairs and undressed in the bathroom and had a shower. When I went into the bedroom, Rex wasn't there and the bed hadn't been disturbed. He's been dreadfully worried about something for months and he hasn't been sleeping well. He often tries to relax by taking a late-night swim in the pool, so I went looking for him. I don't know how long he'd been dead when I found him there.'

'Why didn't you tell the police you didn't get in until after one?'

Her lips were trembling now and the big dark eyes were brimming with tears. 'I wish I had. I wish to God I had. But there were . . . are . . . other problems, and I just let it ride.'

'Other problems?'

'I didn't call them straight away. It was well after two before I phoned.'

She swallowed the last of her drink. I didn't wait for the whip to crack this time. I went over to the drinks tray and poured her a few more opticfuls. I figured Vivian could always charge the booze to the next shampoo-and-set.

Mona gave me a grateful little smile when I handed back her glass, then went on, 'Do you remember, when I came to see you yesterday, I said Rex had been worried about

70

something? Well, I'm pretty sure his Marbella time-share flats project was just a ruse to raise money. He borrowed more than a million pounds from some businessmen, but he didn't buy the land or build the flats. He used it for something else, or invested it, or salted it away somewhere; I don't know which.'

'And?'

'The men he'd borrowed from were threatening him. They came to the house. I heard him having dreadful rows with them over the past month or so. And last night, when I was going into the vicarage, a man we call the major at the bridge club became rather unpleasant. He said I ought to know Rex had let him down badly, and that I was to tell Rex he had to come up with the goods or there'd be trouble.'

'Did you tell the police this?'

'Tell them my husband was a cheat and a swindler? How could I, Mr Lomax? Anyway, I thought that if it became known what he'd done, I might lose the house and everything. Ten years of marriage is a long time. I don't want to walk away with absolutely nothing to show for it.'

'But the people he's ripped off won't just go away. They'll get lawyers to claim against the estate.'

'I very much doubt that, Mr Lomax.

71

They're rich, but they're not what you'd call respectable businessmen. Rex told me it was a mixture of tax evasion and money-laundering. I think they'll try and get the money back some other way.' She gave me a scared look when she said that.

I gazed at her for a while across a couple of yards of Vivian's pink Axminster. I didn't intend telling her I'd seen her talking to an old guy outside the vicarage. And I wasn't going to let her know that her late-lamented had called me over the night before because he was scared she might have been grabbed by the people he'd upset.

All the poise and refinement weren't hiding her fear. She kept giving me wide-eyed, scared little looks, and her lips and hands trembled when she took sips at her drink.

'OK,' I said. 'So there are complications, but why didn't you tell the police about coming in late? And why did you wait an hour before you called them in?'

'I was so upset and muddled. And the police frightened me. I just said I'd found him, and they didn't press me for details. They asked me about recent callers. I told them you'd been to see Rex about time-share flats, but they knew you were a private detective and they kept on and on at me about it, asking why you'd really called.'

'And what did you tell them?'

'I went on saying it was time-share flats. That's what Rex told me; that's what *you* told me. I was afraid to tell them I suspected Rex had hired you to watch me because he thought I was having an affair. What would they have made of that, especially if they'd known I didn't get in until after one? When it came to giving them a statement, I said I'd been to the bridge club, but I didn't tell them I was out until the early hours.'

'But why the delay before you phoned the police?' I was looking at her steadily, trying to make some sense of it all. Big empty house, hubby dead in the pool; most widows would have got the law there fast.

'As I told you. I spent time in the shower before I went down to the pool, and after I found Rex I was ages looking for his keys. I wanted to get into the desk and safe and take out any documents.'

'And did you?'

She shook her head. 'I couldn't find the keys. I just cleared up some papers that were scattered around the pool and hid them in a pile of old magazines in the garage, then I phoned the police. Do you . . . do you think they'll know I've misled them?'

I looked at her, thought about Forensics and body temperatures and the cloud of blood I'd watched being slowly sucked down into the filters. The brandy had brought colour to her cheeks, but the trembling that a few moments ago had only touched her lips now gripped her body. It wasn't the time to make her feel more worried and afraid, so I said gently, 'They may realize there are gaps in your statement, Mrs Saunders. If they press you, just put it down to shock. Tell them you were upset and couldn't think straight. Let them make what they want of that. If they start pressing you about times, just tell them you're confused and can't remember. And go to your doctor as soon as you can. Get some pills for depression, stress: anything that would convince the police that the shock is driving you crazy.'

She rewarded me with a bleak little smile, then sipped the brandy some more. Neither of us spoke for a while. The heat from the fire soaked into my shins while she gave me nervous little looks with big scared eyes. I let my gaze wander over expensive serviceable shoes, mud-splattered silk stockings, rounded knees peeping out from beneath the hem of her skirt, the narrow shoulders that somehow made her look fragile and vulnerable despite her emphatic figure. Looking at her was much more than pleasant; I was enjoying it too much.

Presently I said, 'And where were you until one in the morning, Mrs Saunders?'

'Does it matter?'

'Sure it matters. You want to hire me; I need to know what there is to know, so I can decide whether or not I want to be hired.'

'I promised I wouldn't tell.' Her voice was almost a whisper.

'I'm very discreet.'

'A promise is still a promise.'

I put my glass on the hearth and growled, 'Your husband's been murdered, Mrs Saunders. By all accounts he's taken some hardcases to the cleaners for a million pounds. You've been less than frank with the police. If you want me to help, don't go all coy about telling me where you were the night he died.'

She looked down at her glass. 'I was here with Vivian. Rex had been irritable and distant for months. I knew he had worries, but he didn't have to treat me the way he did. He'd hired you to spy on me, and he hadn't confided in me about his problems. After the bridge club, I couldn't face going home to sit there with Rex ignoring me and being so snappy. So I drove around for a while, feeling sorry for myself, then went to my friend's flat to make myself a hot drink. She's teaching in France at the moment and I've been keeping an eye on the place for her. I remembered that Vivian lives over the precinct, too, so I phoned him and he invited me round. I know he's not your type of man, Mr Lomax, but he's sensitive and kind and easy to talk to. And I needed someone gentle and sympathetic, not some great hairy brute with wandering hands and a onetrack mind.'

'And after a couple of hours of the tea-and-sympathy treatment, you drove yourself home?'

She frowned at me. 'Must you always make those silly remarks? Of course I drove home.'

I smiled at her. She seemed too upset and confused to go on trying to make me feel like the hired hand, for the time being anyway.

'I'm sorry, Mrs Saunders, but you need a lawyer, not a private investigator. My advice is to find one, tell him what you've told me, and then do what he says.'

'Wouldn't he advise me to tell the police everything?'

'Probably.'

'But they'd start digging into Rex's finances, and heaven knows where that would leave me. And they'd think I'd been out on some assignation. Your involvement would convince them I was having an affair, and they could get to thinking I'd had something to do with Rex's death. Anyway, it would implicate Vivian, and I promised I wouldn't mention I'd been with him. He's much too sensitive to cope with the police.'

My smile widened at that. I was pretty sure Vivian was the kind of guy who'd cheerfully flounce his way through almost anything. He might even get a thrill from a bit of rough handling by the boys in blue. And all he'd have to do was confirm Mona's story.

She didn't like the smile. Her lips tightened and she gave an exasperated little snort. 'Really, Mr Lomax, you're so much like my husband: low on tenderness and sensitivity, high on testosterone and hostility. A woman can get very tired of that sort of thing, you know.'

I was laughing softly now. I eased myself to the front of the sofa and began to rise to my feet. 'I think we ought to leave it at that, Mrs Saunders. If you get really abusive, I might get too scared to go home in the dark.'

'Stop making fun of me, and stop saying those stupid things. Help me. Please, Mr Lomax, help me.' She was begging now.

'Take my advice, get a lawyer.'

'A lawyer can't do anything without documents and papers. At least help me get the papers from the desk and safe.'

'If you can't find the keys, you'll need a box man for a job like that.'

'Box-man?'

'Safe-cracker.'

She shook her head. 'I've got the keys.'

'But you said . . . '

'I said I didn't find them before the police came. When I went upstairs later, I saw Rex had left them in the bathroom with things he'd emptied from his pockets when he changed.'

'Then all you've got to do is go up to the house and take what you want.'

'I can't. Not after Rex was murdered there. And I'm too scared of the police and the men Rex cheated.' Her eyes searched my face and her voice took on a wheedling tone as she added, 'I'll pay you well, Mr Lomax. And if you find out what Rex did with the million, I'll double what he offered you.'

She rose to her feet and came close to me. We were almost touching. The warmth of her body was sending out fragrant waves. I could smell the brandy on her breath, see the tracery of fine lines at the corner of her eyes that was saying she wasn't a girl any more. 'Please help me . . . *Please*.'

Persuaded, manipulated, conned, suckered: it doesn't matter what you call it. When she got up close and looked at me like that, my brains slipped into neutral and my mouth went into overdrive. I heard myself saying, 'OK, Mrs Saunders, I'll get the papers from the house for you, but then you've got to find yourself a lawyer.'

7

I parked the car inside the gateway to a field, and began to walk along a hedgerow, putting some distance between me and the road. The rain had stopped, but the night was coaxing a faint mist from sodden earth and grass. After a hundred yards or so, I reached a swathe of woodland which marked the inner boundary of the field, then turned up the slope towards the back garden of Ravenstone House.

There was no moon, and I kept stumbling in the darkness. About half-way up the rise, I stopped and listened, heard dogs snarling and barking beyond the wood, the sound of water dripping from the leaves and branches of trees, my own heavy breathing. I walked on.

A couple of strands of barbed wire and a hawthorn hedge separated the field from the Saunders' place. I slid under the wire, found a gap in the hedge and squeezed through. I could just make out the house now; an angular darkness against a sky that was lit only by stars. I forced my way between shrubs and crossed lawns, moving closer.

I crept down the side of the house, along the blind wall of the swimming pool, until I came to the enclosed yard. I paused for a moment. Dogs were still barking beyond the wood, and the distant muttering of a train was fading into the stillness. I padded across the yard, got out the bunch of keys Mona had given me, and shone my torch on the door. I wasn't going to need a key; someone had taken a jemmy to it. The frame was splintered and it was hanging open. I doused the light, held my breath, listened to the silence for a while, then stepped into the house.

I crossed the kitchen. Through an open door on the far side I could make out vague shapes of furniture in the lounge beyond. The squeak of a rubber sole on polished boards pulled me up short. I listened some more, heard faint sounds of movement: cloth brushing on cloth, the chink of metal.

I leant through the doorway. From where I was standing I could see behind the curving stone wall that formed the island fireplace. A guy was crouching alongside a safe that had been sunk into the floor, his features a vague grey blur in the reflected glow of a pencil flash. He seemed to be completely engrossed. I watched him tinker with the lock for a while, then he put down a tool, tugged at the handle, and lifted a heavy door out of the hole. He got down on his knees, stiffly, as if he'd lingered too long in a crouching

81

position. Then he got his head and the pencil flash closer to the safe.

I drifted into the room, moved around the front of the massive free-standing fireplace and looked back at him from the other side. He was groping around, head down, peering into the hole. I took a ball-point from my breast-pocket and crept closer. When I was three paces away I tossed the pen over his head, back towards the kitchen door. It clattered on the panelling. His whole body jerked and his head thudded against metal as he turned to look towards the sound. I moved in fast, smashed him behind the ear with the heavy rubber torch. He dropped, face down, without a sound.

I laid my fingers on his throat. His pulse was strong. I rolled him over on to his back, shone the torch into his face. Wiry black hair, long sideburns, tanned outdoor features and a moustache that wrapped itself like a dying rodent around a shapeless mouth. His eyes were closed. It was no one I recognized. He was wearing a black tracksuit and black trainers. I checked his pockets. No cash, no identification: nothing.

A glance at the safe door told me he wasn't a professional. The lock was a mess where he'd worked on it. There was a heavy-duty drill, a big jemmy and a clutter of tools in a canvas holdall on the floor beside him. I dragged him clear, then peered inside the safe and saw a couple of leather-covered boxes, a cash book and some bundles of papers. There was too much to carry loose. I went round the front of the fireplace, grabbed a cushion from a chair, unzipped the cover, then went back and crammed the contents of the safe into it.

The man in black was still out cold, so I made for the rear of the house and went into Saunders's tiny study-cum-office. I drew the curtains, closed the door and switched on the light. The desk was a new-looking simulated rosewood creation with a green leather top that had nothing on it but an ashtray and rubber bands and some pencils in a cigar box with no lid.

I slid open drawers, found a half-full bottle of White Horse, four or five boxes of big expensive cigars, some pads of paper and envelopes. It was all pretty tidy. He obviously hadn't had the desk long. The right-hand bottom drawer was locked. I worked my way through the likely-looking keys on the bunch and presently found one that fitted. I pulled the drawer open, lifted out all the papers and stuffed them into the cushion-cover.

I figured the guy I'd left by the safe might be getting ready to make a comeback, so I took a last glance around the room, then switched off the light and went out.

The amateur box-man was still nuzzling the parquet. I played the torch on the side of his face and tried to order my thoughts. I knew I should be searching the place closer than a monkey grooming its mate for fleas, but that would have taken a lot of time, and all Mona Saunders had asked me to do was collect papers from the desk and safe. I prodded the guy with my toe. He groaned. I tried to decide whether or not to call the police and ask them to pick him up. That would have meant a lot of hassle for Mona; me too, if I didn't clear out before they arrived.

A fireproof door at the end of a passage off the hall led into the triple garage. I went through, worked a switch, and half a dozen fluorescent strips flickered then glared off the roof of Saunders's blue Bentley. The magazines were stacked close to the farthermost up-and-over door, just as Mona had said. I went across, leafed through them, found the manila folder of soggy papers she'd salvaged from the poolside, and crammed it into my makeshift sack. I turned off the lights and headed back to the house.

He was moaning now. I could hear it as I moved across the hall. I went into the lounge, grabbed him under the arms, dragged him out through the front door and a good way down the fancy paved driveway. I didn't see a car: maybe he'd been worried about the place being watched and had parked off the premises, like me.

Back in the house, I headed across the hall and into the kitchen. I wedged a chair under the handle of the jemmied back door, grabbed the cushion-cover stuffed with papers and slipped out the front way. It was too dark to see the man dressed in black, but curses were mingling with the groans that were floating down the drive.

It was all downhill after I'd cleared the garden, and a sprint across the field got me back to the car. Breathing hard, I dumped the papers in the boot, slid behind the wheel, got the window down and listened. Dogs were still barking somewhere over the hill, but that was all. No shouting, no engine noise.

I remembered Saunders telling me the road beyond his place ended in a farm. If the guy back at the house had come by car, he'd have to pass my gateway to get back to the main road. I eased off the brake, rolled a little farther back into the field, and waited.

After what seemed an age I heard the clatter of a starter followed by a chorus of frenzied howling from the dog pack. The sound of an engine came closer, lights stabbed the darkness beyond the gateway, and a mud-splattered Volvo estate rumbled past. I gave him enough time to clear the next bend, then motored after him without lights, doing my best to keep the red pin-pricks in view and the Jaguar from riding the verge.

The main Barfield Road was a ribbon of light up ahead. He made a left, heading for town. Traffic was sparse, so I kept well back as we motored through shopping and commercial areas. Then he led me over a railway bridge and down dimly lit brick and concrete canyons that meandered between derelict factories and warehouses. The road dipped under arches, began to run through a rubble-strewn wasteland, past used-car lots and scrapyards. Up ahead, a filling station was challenging the darkness with its glaring light. He turned just after it, down by the canal. I followed.

The road surface was bad now, and streetlamps were wide-spaced and low-powered. I was hanging back as much as I dared. When I rounded the next bend, he'd vanished. Slowing down, I glanced through the only opening. Red tail-lights were jerking up and down: a car was being driven hard over rutted ground.

I cruised on for a few hundred yards, then

turned and headed back. High wooden gates were closing. As I swept past, the two leaves came together and completed the message: 'TULLEY AND SONS — SCRAP METAL MERCHANTS'.

★ ★ ★

I cooked breakfast, ate it standing up, straight out of the pan. It was 9.30 and the sun was busy drying rain from bungalow roofs. The police had given the place a thorough turning-over when they'd searched it. Clearing up the mess had taken almost an hour.

I drank a cup of coffee, then called the number Mona Saunders had given me. The chirp-chirp came down the line for quite a while before I hung up the receiver and went into the bedroom to get my jacket. Then the phone began to shrill, and I went back to the hall and picked it up.

'Paul, where the devil are you? Why aren't you here?' It was Melody. She sounded more agitated than a canary in a cats' home.

'The police searched the bungalow yesterday. I'm just checking things over and clearing up the mess.'

'Well, you'd better get over here right away, because they're ransacking your office now.'

I winced at that, and a vague worry I

87

couldn't identify began to fret away at the edges of my mind. I instinctively slid my hand inside my jacket. The empty pocket told me what the trouble was. I'd slid Saunders's chequebook under the blotter on my desk when Vivian Delmar paid me a call the night before.

'Paul . . . Paul, are you still there?'

'Sure, I'm here.' I was busy trying to goad the half-dozen brain cells I do my thinking with into action. Making my voice urgent, I said, 'Be an angel and do me a great big favour.'

'Don't angel me because you want something. You're in trouble, aren't you?'

'Nothing we can't handle.'

'We? Who said anything about we?' The husky voice was indignant.

'There's a chequebook, a big blue chequebook, under the blotter on the desk. The police mustn't find it.'

'They probably already have. Two of them have been up there quite a while.'

'Look,' I urged, 'go up to the office: distract them, get their attention off the job and grab the book.'

'Don't be ridiculous. I can't do that.'

'Nobody could do it better, angel. When you walk in, they won't be able to tear their eyes off you.'

'But what if they see me taking it?'

'Just smile and tell them it's yours.'

'You're mad, you know that? Quite mad.'

She put the phone down on me. I listened to the faint buzzing on the line for a few moments, then pressed the studs in the cradle and dialled the flat where Mona Saunders was staying. No one answered.

8

I could hear Melody's husky laughter and Mace's Cockney baritone, as I crossed the waiting-room. I stepped into the office. Melody was sitting on the desk, hands cupped around a raised knee. The hem of her cream skirt had ridden up, exposing plenty of thigh. Her lips were parted in a radiant smile and her shoulders were thrown well back. I guess she was showing Mace what she could do for the mulberry sweater.

She glanced towards me, put on a breathless, sexy little voice as she said, 'You're dreadfully late, Paul. I didn't think you were coming in. You're being searched. I've told them you never keep records and all they'll find are empty whisky bottles and old socks, but they don't believe me.'

'I'm beginning to.' A shirt-sleeved cop sifting through a wodge of dusty papers in a cupboard said that.

'Chief Inspector Mace has been telling me all about his job and the arrests he's made. It's been absolutely fascinating,' she gushed.

Mace stopped scowling at me and his pasty

features worked into a smile again as his gaze moved back to Melody. She'd promoted him to Chief Inspector. He liked it. He liked it a lot.

'You got a warrant?' I growled.

Talking to me was the last thing on his mind. He couldn't drag his eyes off the vision on the desk. Melody gazed right back at him from under long lashes, her lips shaped into a provocative little smile.

'Yeah, I've got a warrant,' he said.

'Maybe I could see it, just for the record?'

He pushed himself off the filing cabinet, sauntered over, handed me a slip of paper. 'Don't go all smart on me and start whining about your rights, Lomax, or I might just start exercising mine.'

I unfolded it. It all seemed OK. I knew it would.

As I handed it back, I heard the clatter of cups and glanced towards Melody. She was stacking crockery on to a tray. I could see the big blue chequebook peeping out from under the coffee pot.

'I'll have to leave you now,' she said. Then, looking at Mace, she put a lot of feeling into her voice as she added, 'You're terribly brave, Inspector, dealing with such vicious criminals.'

Mace leered. He was lapping it up. 'All in a

day's work, darling, and I'm even better off duty.'

'Mmm, I bet you are,' she breathed, then hoisted up the tray and strutted out, her heels tap-tapping over the linoleum in the waiting-room.

Mace's eyes lingered on the neat little posterior she was waving around. When she disappeared through the outer door, he turned and looked at me, switched off the smile and switched on the hard-cop look.

'You're a slovenly sod, Lomax. There's nothing but trash in this stinking rat-trap.' He glanced over his shoulder. 'Get the desk done now, Foster.'

The shirt-sleeved cop who'd been sifting through dusty papers slammed the cupboard door shut, then went over and started rummaging on the desk.

Mace looked back at me. 'I think you're holding out on us, Lomax, and I don't like that.'

I leant against the door-frame, folded my arms and gave him a genial look. 'Holding out?'

'Yeah, holding out. Saunders hires you and gets mangled; the next day, you're working for the widow.'

'Who says so?'

'She says so. We took her in. Eight this

92

morning. She kept whimpering for you. She didn't want a lawyer, just you.'

'Why take Mona Saunders in?'

Mace grinned and gave me a knowing look. 'We think *she's* holding out on us, too.'

I held his gaze and said nothing.

'It doesn't gel,' Mace said. 'He was dead two, maybe three hours before she called us. But then, you know that, don't you, Lomax?'

'All I know is time-share flats.'

'You say time-share flats once more and I'll pull you in!'

We did some more eye-wrestling. Presently I said, 'So what? Maybe she just thought he was out and went to bed. It's a big house. You wouldn't expect her to check everything before she turned in.'

'Vicar says she left the bridge club around nine. She could have been home around 9.15, almost three hours before Saunders bought it.'

'Maybe you've got the time of death wrong. Maybe it was while she was playing a rubber with the vicar.'

'Forensics say eleven at the earliest, one at the latest, and they're pretty sure about this one.'

'She didn't do it. She's not the type.'

'Yeah, I think she's gorgeous, too,' he sneered. 'It takes all kinds, Lomax: pretty and plain. She could have done it, or someone could have done it for her, or because of her. Maybe that's where *you* come in. Maybe Saunders wanted a transom-peeper because Mona was a two-timing bitch.'

I looked at him, tried to work out why a truculent cop was telling me all this. Out loud I said, 'Are you arresting her?'

'Not yet. She's just helping with enquiries at the moment.'

He glanced over his shoulder towards the desk. 'You finished, Foster?'

'Just about.'

Mace looked back at me. 'Why did Saunders hire you, Lomax? And why is his wife saying you're representing her now he's dead?'

'I don't care what she told you, it's me that decides who I represent or don't represent.'

'Word's out that Saunders had some pretty big chickens coming home to roost. If you're wise, you'll get the hell out of it before they climb up on their perch and crap all over you.'

'Chickens?'

He grinned at me. 'You ought to carry a brain donor card, Lomax. You're so smart, mankind couldn't stand the loss if you got mangled.'

His partner was pulling on a car coat.

Mace glanced at him, then motioned towards the door and said, 'Come on, Foster, let's get some fresh air.'

I listened to them laughing their way down the stairs. When I couldn't hear them any more I went over to the desk and lifted out the office bottle, swallowed a mouthful of the amber spirit, and stood there while the warm reviving glow spread through me.

The phone began to ring. I hoisted the receiver.

'Mr Lomax?'

'Speaking.' Getting a 'mister' was a big ego massage these days.

'I understand you were retained by the late Rex Saunders.' The man had a clipped, very top-drawer kind of voice.

'Why should that concern you?'

'I think we may be able to help one another.'

'And who would I be helping?'

'Sorry, old boy. Name's Maslow, Frederick Maslow.'

'How would I be helping you, Mr Maslow?'

'Don't like doing business over the phone, old boy. Come up to the house and we'll talk over a drink.'

'Rex Saunders is dead, Mr Maslow. As far as I'm concerned, any business I had with him is finished.'

'Not finished, just beginning. Come up to the house. It really would be worth your while.'

'We must have a bad line. I said finished and I meant finished. There's no point my seeing you.'

'Nonsense, old boy. I'll send a car. Have it there in twenty minutes.' He rang off.

I slammed the phone down, headed out and made for the ground floor. Through Melody's reception window I could see three or four girls pecking away at keyboards, staring glassy-eyed into monitors. A lissom number with short black hair glanced up. I mouthed the word 'Melody'. Without faltering on the keys, she inclined her head towards the far end of the room.

I went on in, made my way between the desks towards an inner office. I stepped inside and closed the door. Melody was bending over the desk, a wave of blonde hair brushing her cheek. She was flicking through a card index in a shallow metal tray.

She glanced up. When she saw it was me, she scowled and her voice wasn't friendly when she said, 'Don't you dare ask me to do anything like that again, Paul.'

I flopped down on the visitors' chair and grinned up at her. 'I knew your legs were great, but I'd no idea they were sensational.'

She blushed. 'Don't, Paul. It's bad enough having to act the tart for you, without having to listen to your puerile remarks.'

'Puerile?'

'Silly, immature and trivial. I think that just about sums up most of the things you say.'

I laughed gently; watched her trying hard not to smile. 'Did you get the book?'

She tugged at a drawer, pulled out the blue chequebook and tossed it towards me. I caught it.

'How did you make out?'

She brushed the stray lock of hair away from her face, and went on searching through the cards as she said, 'After you phoned, I took coffee up, put the tray on the desk and served it. I could see the corner of the chequebook sticking out from underneath the blotter, so I just sat on it and simpered. They lapped it up.'

'Simpered?' I let my grin broaden.

'Yes, simpered,' she snapped.

'And you sat on the book?'

'That's what I've just said, isn't it?'

I gave the chequebook a lingering kiss.

Her blush deepened. She wasn't managing to hide the smile now. 'Really, Paul, they ought to put you in a zoo.'

'Would you come and visit me?'

'I'd come and rattle the bars of your cage,' she said.

She plucked a card out of the index, moved back to the desk, then asked, 'What's so special about the chequebook, anyway?'

'It belonged to Saunders. He's been murdered. One of the stubs has my name on it.'

She gave me a worried, searching kind of look. 'You're in trouble again, aren't you?'

'Nothing I can't handle.' I grinned and put a conviction I didn't feel into the words.

She was close enough for me to catch her perfume. I let my eyes browse over her, gave them a roller-coaster ride on curves that put my pulse rate up and left me a little breathless. Perched on the desk in that pin-up pose, she'd have mesmerized Mace so completely she'd have been able to walk out with his vest and pants without him noticing.

There was a knock at the door and a girl with greasy skin and a weight problem came through.

' 'Scuse me,' she said. 'There's two men in the hall asking for Mr Lomax. They said they'd been sent by a man called Maslow.'

★   ★   ★

98

Dark bespoke-tailored suits weren't hiding the heavy muscular frames of the two guys in the hall. Their bored, disinterested eyes watched me as I walked towards them.

'Mr Lomax?' The taller of the two asked.

'That's me.'

'Mr Maslow sent the car for you.' He glanced through the open entrance door.

I followed his gaze. A big black limousine, the kind of thing you only get to ride in at funerals, had been driven up the pedestrianized area and parked at the bottom of the steps. I could see a grey-uniformed chauffeur behind the wheel.

'I told Maslow I didn't want to see him.'

'We don't know anything about that, Mr Lomax. We just came to escort you back to the house.'

'Well, you can escort one another. You've wasted your time.'

They closed in with their taut, no-nonsense faces and slid their arms through mine.

'Mr Maslow won't keep you long, Mr Lomax,' said the shorter man. He was a Scot.

I opened my mouth to do some more arguing, then decided against it and forced myself to relax.

'OK,' I said wearily, 'take me to your leader.'

9

Maslow's place wasn't much bigger than Barfield's best hotel. Fancy chimneys, stucco, oak beams, windows with tiny leaded panes: a classy stockbroker's Tudor pile set on a rise and overlooking the valley to the south of town. Time had mellowed the bricks and timber and tiles; made the Edwardian evocation seem a little less of a pastiche, a little more Tudor-like.

The chauffeur let the limousine roll to a stop beneath a downward-sweeping projection of the main roof which was carried on a row of brick barley-sugar columns. My escorts climbed out. I followed. The car pulled away and swept around the back of the house. We climbed, three abreast, up wide stone steps. The one with the Scottish accent opened the massive iron-bound oak door and we all piled into the entrance hall.

I gazed around while we waited. The place was about thirty feet square and oak panelled up to a delft rail that carried an assortment of oriental plates. Crimson carpet cascaded down an impressive flight of stairs and extended, in a river of red, over polished oak boards to the front door.

The only furniture was a refectory table beside a door in the far wall. On the table was a blue-glazed Chinese dragon about a yard high.

I heard footsteps, the door opened and a woman of around twenty-five came through. She was tall, maybe six feet in her high-heels. Her features were fine and regular, but some distance this side of beautiful. Her flawless skin was like brownish-black velvet.

'This is Mr Lomax, Gloriana. Mr Maslow said he had to be taken straight through.'

She played her big brown eyes on me and her teeth showed startling white as she murmured, 'Follow me, please, Mr Lomax.' The way she said those five little words told me we'd been born and bred within shouting distance of one another.

She led me down the hall, through a door at the side of the stairs and along a corridor where some more of the crimson carpet was wall-to-wall and the oak panelling was floor-to-ceiling. Her long-sleeved light-grey dress had a white collar and cuffs. There was no bib to her tiny white apron. Her high heels were rock steady, the seams of her stockings as straight as Cupid's arrows. The gentle rhythm of her hips had set the flared hem of her skirt swaying. It was short enough for me to see the dark hollows behind her knees. I guess upstairs maids are an endangered species these days. This tall, slender, ebony job must have been unique. Six feet of slinky sensuality any mistress of the house would be wise to do without.

We made a right into a wider corridor, and she stopped and tapped gently on the first door we came to. I heard a harsh voice bellow, 'Enter.' She took me inside and said softly, 'Mr Lomax, sir.'

'Thanks, Gloriana. You can leave us now.'

The man who'd said that rose from a chair and came towards me between black lacquered chinoiserie tables littered with bronze and jade ornaments that were so grotesque I guessed they had to be priceless. His hands were thrust into the pockets of his tweed jacket, thumbs hooked over the tops.

'Thanks for coming, old boy. I'm grateful, dashed grateful. Come on in and sit yourself down.' He jerked out a hand. I grasped it. The shaking that followed was brisk and vigorous.

His thin lips were like the healing edges of a long scar. When he spoke, he opened his mouth wide and his ultra-refined voice was harsh and clipped, as if it had been fed through a loudhailer. Close-cropped white hair and icy-blue eyes stood out against a ruddy complexion. He had a beaked nose and his massive, protruding chin was frosted over with white stubble. It was the guy I'd seen talking to Mona outside the vicarage.

We moved over to a pair of leather armchairs set in a bay window that was big enough to garage a bus.

'Drink?'

'I'd appreciate that.'

'What'll you have, old boy? Gin, brandy, Scotch?'

'A Scotch would be fine.'

'Chap after my own heart. Scotch and soda man myself.'

He made for a black laquered cabinet that had fancy hinges and Chinese scenes painted on the doors. I looked around the big, high room. Sunlight was flooding through the mullioned bay, its brilliant intensity revealing that the leather chairs and sofas and Persian carpets were no longer new. Oil paintings of hunting-dogs and wild-fowl lined the pale-green walls. The fireplace on my left was a grotesquely carved black oak and bottle-green tiled monstrosity that rose up through the full height of the room. Set into a panel in the upper half was a painting of a stag held at bay by a pack of snarling hounds.

I heard a voice saying something to me, and turned and looked at Maslow again.

'Anything with it?'

'Just as it is.'

He brought me a good measure over in a chunk of Waterford crystal. He was big boned and broad shouldered, with tiny blue eyes that were clear and shrewd. I guessed he was in his late fifties and still the strong, vigorous, outdoor type. He sat down in the chair facing mine. When he crossed his cavalry twills I saw he was wearing brown boots.

He raised his glass, barked, 'Cheers, old boy,' and downed a mouthful. Then he flashed me a sly, man-of-the-world grin, and gold glittered amongst stumpy, tobacco-stained teeth.

I was feeling angry. It might have been his whisky, but it was my time he was wasting. I let it sound in my voice when I said, 'Your men wouldn't take no for an answer when they collected me, Mr Maslow. Could we get this over with so they can take me back?'

His grin widened. 'Certainly, old boy. Time's money. Saunders, Rex Saunders: you were working for him. Now you've been engaged by his wife.'

I eyed him steadily. The grin seemed to be frozen on to his face. First the cops, now Maslow. It would have been clear to the cops I was working for Mona when she asked for me instead of a lawyer. I couldn't figure out

104

how Maslow knew. Maybe he was just probing. It worried me.

I said, 'Saunders is dead. I can't do business with a dead man. I'm not working for his widow.'

'That's not what I'm told.'

'Then you've been told wrong.'

'For the money I pay, old boy, I'm never told wrong.'

I took a first sip at my glass and studied his gaunt, florid features. Presently I said, 'How could my involvement with Rex Saunders possibly interest you, Mr Maslow?'

'I lent him money; invested it with him. Now that he's dead, it could be difficult for me to get it back.'

'Surely you can claim against his estate?'

'Can't. Not that sort of deal, old boy. It was money I couldn't put through the books. I had to get it off my hands for a while. Tax, you understand. He needed cash for a building project, so I lent him the lot on the promise of a slice of the profits. Gentleman's agreement. No paperwork, no receipts.'

'Gentleman's agreement?' Surprise registered in my voice. He didn't look the type.

'Sounds naïve, but I knew old Rex pretty well. Built me a pool here a couple of years ago; built pools or fancy extensions on most of the houses around here. He was doing well. Got the knack of turning a pound into a tenner and doing it pretty damn quick.' He gulped at his drink, swallowed noisily. 'Anyway, I liked him, dammit. He was a decent sort. And I'd no alternative: I had to offload the cash for a while, and Rex promised a good return on it. No point letting it mark time in a safe deposit box. We'd been helping one another in that way for a year or more. No names, no pack drill, no papers, no tax. Never let him have as much as that before, though.'

'How much was involved?'

He gave me a resigned look. 'Just short of half a million. He needed it to get some time-share flats project off the ground in Marbella. Sounded a good scheme.'

'You've been surprisingly frank, Mr Maslow.'

'There's only the two of us here. I'd deny every word and then make sure your mouth stayed shut.' He laughed. 'You're discreet, aren't you, old boy? Rex was shrewd. If *he* could trust you, I'm sure I can.'

'And where does all this get us, Mr Maslow?'

'Obvious, old boy. You're working for the widow: her hubby had my cash. I can't think of anyone better placed to help me get it back.'

106

'If I am working for Mona Saunders, there could be a conflict of interests.'

'Don't see how. Money isn't hers. All Rex did was get some fancy architect to do a few drawings. Never even bought the site. I contacted a land agent in Spain to check that out a month ago. That's what started the alarm bells ringing. Tackled old Rex about it two or three times. Now some silly beggar's killed him.'

'What makes you think I'm working for the widow?'

He tapped the side of his hooked nose with a nicotine-stained finger and gave me a sly little grin. 'You're not the only one who can be discreet, old boy. I know you're working for her, and I'm pretty sure you got some papers out of the house for her last night.'

I took a pull at the whisky, forced myself to return his grin, said, 'For once you've got it wrong, Mr Maslow. I'm not working for Mona Saunders, and I don't know anything about any papers.'

'Wouldn't expect you to say anything else, but I know you're working for the widow and I'm certain it was you who chopped Andrew's boy when he'd got his hands in the safe.'

'Andrew's boy?'

'Tulley, Andrew Tulley: scrap metal man. He put up the rest of the cash. His boy went to see what he could find at the house, and some blighter clobbered him, cleaned the place out and dumped him on the drive. And we both know who did that, don't we, Lomax?' He was grinning at me again.

'Sounds far-fetched to me. Why didn't Mona Saunders get the papers herself? And why don't you and this Tulley guy just go and see her and tell her you want your money back?'

'Tried it, old boy. Day after Rex died. Didn't like doing it, but half a million is half a million, dammit. She said she didn't know a thing about it, said Rex didn't tell her anything about the business, and made out she'd no ready cash, just the house and the cars. Tulley didn't believe a word of it, but I think she was telling the truth. Why else would she have hired you, if it wasn't to recover the cash?' He eyed me for a while, then said, 'Well?'

'Well what, Mr Maslow?'

'Well, are we going to do business? I'm prepared to pay your usual daily rates, plus one per cent of whatever you recover. One per cent of half a million is a tidy sum. Think about it, Mr Lomax.'

'I've thought about it, and the answer's no.'

He scowled. Bushy white eyebrows dropped like snowfalls from a rocky ledge. He wasn't grinning now. 'You're a choosy beggar, Lomax. Saunders is dead. It's *my* money. I'm offering you your usual rates, plus a one per cent recovery bonus. Why the devil won't you take the job?'

I looked him straight in the eye while I groped for a convincing reason. Even if I kissed Mona Saunders goodbye when I handed over the sack full of papers, I couldn't just join the other team and help them move in on her. And how was I to know all this no-paperwork unsecured loan crap Maslow was giving me was the truth? But there were other reasons for my backing-off; reasons I couldn't quite flesh-out with words. First of all there was the faint little voice warning me to get the hell out of it: the same voice I'd not listened to when I'd taken the job from Saunders and when I'd let Mona hire me. I felt like a wasp stuck in honey. I recalled my first meeting with Saunders, and a picture of Mona climbing out of the pool flooded my mind. I realized then what all the other reasons were: realized who was the honey.

I said, 'I didn't want the job when Saunders persuaded me to take it, and the police haven't left me alone since he died. Your offer's generous, Mr Maslow, but I'm going to have to turn you down. I guess you'll have to find another agency.'

'I want *you*, Mr Lomax.' His voice was low, almost menacing.

'I specialize in commercial work. Another agency would do you a better job.'

'But you have something they don't.'

I raised an eyebrow.

'Papers, old boy. Rex Saunders's papers. And there's something else: I know you're discreet. That's very important to me.'

I grinned at him. 'You've been told wrong about the papers, old boy.'

He scowled and his long scar of a mouth almost healed. He wasn't used to being turned down. Most of all, he wasn't used to being taunted about his verbal mannerisms.

I heard a knocking on the door. He ignored it, just went on glowering at me.

The knocking sounded again, quicker, more insistent.

He dragged his narrowed eyes off mine, glared at the door and barked, 'Enter.'

The black maid cruised in. 'Sorry to disturb you, sir, but Kelly's worried about the dog.'

'Worried? What the devil does that mean, dammit?'

'It's in a frenzy . . . It's gone crazy. He's worried about its teeth.'

'Teeth?'

'It's chewing at the bars, walls, floor,

110

everything, sir. Kelly thinks it might — '

'I'm coming, Gloriana. Tell him I'm coming.'

She hurled a 'Very good, sir,' at him over her shoulder as she ran out.

He looked back at me, his anger apparently forgotten. 'Don't object to bloodsports, do you, Mr Lomax?'

I was going to repeat Oscar Wilde's crack about the unspeakable pursuing the uneatable, thought better of it, and said, 'So long as it's not me the hounds are chasing.'

He gave a throaty chuckle. 'That's the spirit. Come and take a look at the dog. I'll bet you've never seen anything like him.'

I could hear the growling and snarling as we crossed the yard. Maslow pushed open a door and I followed him into a place that had probably been used as a laundry when the house was first built. A cage of heavy steel bars sealed off one end.

The thing beyond the bars had a huge head and a powerful, barrel-chested body. Wiry black hair gleamed and wicked jaws that seemed to have a double ration of teeth were clamped on one of the bars. It was snarling and slobbering, trying to chew its way through the steel.

Maslow went up to the cage. 'What's the matter, Sting, boy? What the devil's the matter?' His voice was as soothing as acid in a cut. He was almost yelling the words to make himself heard.

The dog ignored him.

Maslow grabbed a broom, tried to push the dog off the bars. It made a grab for the handle, got it in its jaws, began to jerk it around, grinding and crunching it into a splintered mess. Maslow struggled to pull the broom free, dragged the dog's snout between the bars. I saw then that its head and back were terribly scarred and carried the marks of crude stitching. Its left eye was white and opaque; one of its ears was half torn away.

Sting let go of the broom handle and Maslow staggered back to a crescendo of frenzied barking.

'Dope some meat,' he snapped.

A short guy in a flannel shirt and baggy corduroy trousers opened a fridge, took out a couple of pounds of steak and threw them down on a wooden table. He grabbed a bottle, shook out a couple of tablets, ground them in the hollow of a spoon and sprinkled the powder over the meat. Then he picked up the bloody flesh and tossed it through the bars.

We stood in silence, watching the dog tear at the raw tissue, dragging chunks into its slobbering jaws, then throwing back its head and swallowing them almost without chewing.

'What do you make of him?' Maslow said.

I glanced up, saw him looking at me, his craggy features arranged in an expression of almost filial pride.

'He's hardly a ladies' lapdog. What's he used for?'

'Fighting,' he said simply. 'Never been beaten. Five kills and heaven knows how many maimings to his credit. Pit bulls, ever heard of them? Had this one flown in from the States. Bred for courage, aggression, ferocity. Makes 'em difficult to handle. This one's getting worse. Too many fights, too many kills. Brute's more deadly than a loaded gun.'

The dog was quieter now. It had gobbled up the meat and was sniffing around for second helpings. Maslow looked at the man in the flannel shirt.

'Stay with him for a while, Kelly,' he said. 'Come and tell me if he goes on being difficult.'

We stepped out into the sunlight. The enclosed yard was trapping its warmth. The chauffeur who'd brought me to the house was polishing the coachwork of the big limousine. He didn't look up as we passed.

'Where do you fight the dogs?' I was only

113

making polite conversation. He could have unleashed them at the vicarage jumble sale for all I cared.

He eyed me shrewdly, then said, 'We've got a pit in a workshop in Tulley's scrap yard. Place is screened from the road by a high wall, out of the way, no houses. Got to be careful, or we'll have the law and the damned animal rights blighters poking their noses in. We've had no trouble so far.'

'You run a club, then?'

'Nothing as formal as that. More a banding together of kindred spirits.'

'Was Rex Saunders involved?'

He shot me a narrow-eyed look. 'Didn't sport a dog, Mona wouldn't have allowed it, but he used to come along and have a wager. Ed Hawkins, the chap who has the farm along the lane from the Saunders' place, breeds them. One of Tulley's sons has a share in the business. Doing quite well. Plenty of enthusiasts keen on the sport. It's always been difficult; with the police, I mean. But it's got worse over the past few years. Law's been tightened, can't get dogs in from the States any more.'

'What's your line of business, Mr Maslow?'

'Meat: wholesale. Buy it on the hoof; sell it by the boatload. Own the abattoir behind the market. That's where my father started out.

Firm's grown a bit since then though.'

We made our way back to the room with the big bay window and stood in front of the monumental eyesore of a fireplace. He was looking at me, hands in his jacket pockets, thumbs hooked over the tops. I wondered if the ultra-refined accent and the brisk military manner were the genuine article or whether it was something he'd had to work hard at.

'Let me get you another drink, old chap.'

I thanked him and declined.

'I'd like you to reconsider my offer before you go.'

'I'm no use to you, Mr Maslow. I'm pretty certain the police think I'm involved in some way in Saunders's death, and that doesn't leave me free to act for you.'

'I'll deal with the police if they're harassing you. And it might be better for the widow if you take the job. Nobody's going to make a fool of me, Mr Lomax. If I find out she's been hiding something, she'll have to be brought to her senses. Someone else might not be quite as gentle with her as you'd be.'

I eyed him steadily, kept quiet, let the words sink in.

He went on, 'Tulley put up the other half-million. He doesn't know it was you who clubbed his son last night. They're a close family. If he finds out you did it, the uncouth

115

beggars will come looking for you. If they think you've any idea where Saunders stashed the cash, they'll beat the living daylights out of you till you tell. And it could be worse for the widow. She's a dashed attractive woman, and they don't even pretend to be gentlemen. Think about that, old boy.'

He strode over to where we'd been sitting, picked up my glass, carried it over to the decanter and recharged it. Maybe he hadn't heard me when I'd said I didn't want a refill. I glanced up at the stag in the picture, muttered, 'You and me both, Rudolph,' then watched him lope back. I took the glass.

'Well?'

'OK, Mr Maslow, I'll see what I can do. But don't get impatient, it could take some time.'

'Good man.' He beamed at me and his gash of a mouth split open. He clinked his glass on mine, downed the spirit in one gulp. I followed suit. I guess I needed it a damned sight more than he did.

'Maybe your driver could run me back to town?'

'Of course.' He pressed a button by the side of the fire-place.

I said, 'Shall I phone you here if I come up with anything?'

He nodded, told me an ex-directory

number, which I took down. 'And for heaven's sake be discreet. When you phone, make sure it's me you're speaking to. Never leave messages. Frankly, old boy, I'm as upset about being made a fool of by Saunders as I am about the money.'

I heard a knocking at the door. Maslow went through his 'Enter' routine and the black maid swirled in.

'Show Mr Lomax to the car, will you, Gloriana? He's leaving now.'

She flashed me a smile. I shook hands with Maslow and she stood aside while I passed through the door.

She walked slightly ahead of me as we moved down the corridor. Her slipstream was fragrant with the smell of soap and clean linen. No perfume. Maybe Maslow couldn't handle the extra stimulation.

I gave her a smile, one of my hundred-kilowatt specials, and said, 'What do you do after you've served afternoon tea?'

She gave me a bored, heard-it-all-before look, and her eyes rolled over me, lazily, from under curling black lashes.

'Get ready to serve dinner,' she said.

'And after you've served dinner?'

'I generally take in the brandy and cigars.'

'Likes a cigar, does she, Mrs Maslow?'

She giggled. 'There is no Mrs Maslow.'

'And after you've taken Mr Maslow his brandy and cigars?'

She was showing me lots of strong white teeth now. She fluttered her lashes and did a near-perfect cotton-picking-mammy imitation as she said, 'Why, massa, Ah guess Ah's jest so pooped out, Ah gits upstairs and flops out on mah little truckle-bed.'

She yanked open the huge front door.

I stepped through and grinned back at her. 'Thanks, Gloriana. Perhaps I could come up and tuck you in sometime; read you a bedtime story? *Uncle Tom's Cabin* maybe, or *Gone With the Wind.*'

The car was waiting. I climbed inside; the chauffeur closed the door. I glanced back up the steps. She was still peeping out and showing me lots of teeth as the limousine whispered off down the drive.

10

When I got back to the office, I dialled Mona Saunders's number. She answered so quickly she must have been sitting with the phone on her lap. I let her know who it was.

'Mr Lomax, thank God it's you.' Her voice was breathless with relief. 'I called you half an hour ago, but your secretary told me you were out. She was very offhand. Is she usually like that?'

I grinned to myself. 'She's not really my secretary, Mrs Saunders. And no, she's not usually like that.'

'The police made me go to their headquarters this morning.'

'I know. A cop called Mace gave me the news while he was ransacking the office.'

'Did you get the papers?'

'Yes, shall I bring them over?'

'To my friend's flat, you mean?'

'Sure, why not?'

'The police . . . Would it be wise?'

'We're not fooling anyone, Mrs Saunders. They know your husband hired me; they know I'm working for you. Everyone in Barfield seems to know our business. I don't see any point in hiding it any more.'

'You know best,' she said. 'When will you come?'

'Now, if that's OK.'

'Have you had lunch?'

I said I hadn't. She said she'd make me some, gave me the address of her friend's flat, told me to head for Vivian's place, then walk around the access deck. I told her I'd be there in fifteen minutes.

★ ★ ★

The steak Mona cooked was big and tender; the coffee hot, fragrant and freshly ground. By the time I'd finished the third cup, I'd forgiven her for telling the police I was representing her; forgiven her for involving me in her personal problems. It wasn't just the steak and the coffee. Her huge dark eyes, the shape of her mouth, the dimples when she gave me those scared little smiles, would have made me forgive and forget almost anything.

She began to clear away the debris of the meal. I relaxed back in a spindly dining-chair, watched her moving between the table and a neat little yellow-and-white kitchen. She was giving a lot of shape to an exclusive-looking bluish-grey silk suit. Her hair fell in dark, shining waves, almost to the hem of the tiny jacket. Her stockings were silvery-blue, her shoes grey crocodile skin. She wasn't wearing any make-up, but I noticed she'd clipped those tiny pearl studs to her ears again.

I tried to organize my thoughts while I listened to cups and plates rattling and water splashing. I could tell from the few words we'd spoken during the meal that she thought she'd hired me. I had to make my mind up fast about whether I was going to be involved or not, and I had to tell her about Maslow's proposition before we opened up the cushion cover stuffed with her husband's papers.

The well-cooked meal and the domestic noises drifting in from the kitchen were making me feel good in spite of the things they reminded me of. I let my eyes wander around the living room of the tiny flat, took in the Mexican style rugs on polished brown tiles, Ercol chairs and table and sideboard made from some honey-coloured wood, the bright travel posters on matt white walls.

Suddenly Mona was standing in the kitchen doorway, drying her hands on a towel and giving me a long, steady look. When she caught my eye, she gave me a frightened little smile.

'Before we go any further, we've got to have a talk,' I said.

She hung the towel behind the door and said, 'About what?' then came over and sat facing me across the circular table.

'About why you told the police you didn't want a lawyer; that I was representing you. When the cops get you, you need a lawyer, Mrs Saunders. A private investigator is no use to you at all.'

She gave me a hurt, bewildered look. 'But I don't know any lawyers. And they were so beastly to me I became completely confused. You were getting the papers for me. I just couldn't think of anyone but you.'

'How were they beastly to you?'

She blushed heavily, looked down at her hands. 'They asked me things, intimate things, about my marriage. And they kept on and on at me about where I was the night Rex died and about the time I got home. I could tell they knew I'd not been completely frank with them about that. They as much as said that if I hadn't shot him, then some man I was having an affair with had. But I'm not having an affair, Mr Lomax, I swear I'm not. I loved Rex. Things hadn't been perfect for a long time, but I knew he had a lot of worries and I was prepared to wait for things to come right again.'

'The cop called Mace told me they picked you up about eight.'

'That's right. A man and a woman. The policewoman stayed in the bedroom while I dressed. It was so embarrassing. I'm sure they're convinced I had something to do with Rex's death. They told me they wanted me back again tomorrow for some more questioning.' Shock and shame and anger mingled in a voice that was tearful now.

'A guy called Maslow sent a car and a couple of minders to collect me this morning. You know anyone by that name?'

She nodded, looked sheepish. 'He's the man we call the major at the bridge club. He was one of the men my husband owed money to.'

'He wants it back.'

'I know. He came to see me at the house, the day after Rex died, with a man called Tulley. They said Rex had borrowed half a million pounds from each of them and they wanted it repaying immediately. I told them I didn't know anything about Rex's business, but I'd look into it when I sorted his affairs out. Mr Maslow was doing his best to be gentlemanly about it, but Tulley was vile. He's a coarse, evil brute. That's one of the reasons why I had to get out of the house. Tulley made some unspeakable threats about what would happen if he didn't get his money back. He embarrassed Mr Maslow. My

123

husband was a very physical man, Mr Lomax, but he was never coarse.'

'Maslow tried to hire me to recover the cash.'

'You . . . You didn't say yes?'

'I couldn't say no. He made it clear that if I didn't take the job, they'd find somebody else who'd get rough with you if you didn't clear the debt.'

'Are you going to help him?'

'Would I be telling you all this if I was?'

She was looking at me wide-eyed now, her face ashen beneath the summer tan.

Presently I said, 'You should get well clear of Barfield. Is there anywhere you can go for a while?'

She didn't answer me, just ran the tip of her tongue around her lips and kept up the wide-eyed stare.

'Your parents, perhaps?' I prompted.

She shook her head. 'My parents are in Ireland. They haven't had anything to do with me since I married Rex. Quite a few of my cousins are priests and nuns, so I suppose marrying a divorced man made me the black sheep of the family. Daddy disowned me. Going home and facing them would be worse than staying here and coping with Rex's creditors. And the police told me not to leave town, so surely they'll protect me.'

'It's not easy to protect anyone from men like Tulley.'

'But you'll protect me, won't you, Mr Lomax?' She was giving me a helpless, dewy-eyed look now. Her parted lips were trembling. I figured it was just another facial arrangement from her man-manipulating repertoire. But she was scared. That was obvious. Judas Priest, I was scared. Who wouldn't have been?

'I take it you don't have any problems with giving Maslow and Tulley their money back, if we find it?'

'Of course not, so long as we can identify it as their money and not part of Rex's estate. If they were stupid enough to lend money without documents to prove it, I don't see why I should sell all I've got to help pay them back.'

'They're shrewd and greedy, Mrs Saunders, and they're not stupid. If we don't come up with the cash, they'll come looking for us.'

'Help me, Mr Lomax.' Her voice was low and her eyes were begging me.

I looked at her. I'd no alternative. I'd allowed myself to become embroiled in the mess and, like her, there was nowhere I could run. I put what warmth I could into my voice and said, 'Sure, Mrs Saunders. I'll help you.'

I shoved my chair back and rose from the

table. 'We'd better give those papers the once-over. I'll go and get them from the car.' When I reached the door, I glanced back at her. She was staring down at her hands. I said, 'I've levelled with you, Mrs Saunders. I hope you're not keeping any secrets from me.'

She jerked her head up and gave me a wounded look. 'I've told you everything, Mr Lomax, absolutely everything.'

★ ★ ★

We spent upwards of an hour sifting through the papers together. The only items that looked promising were a long narrow cash book Saunders seemed to have kept for his own benefit, not the tax-man's, and a small diary that had been mixed up with the papers I'd taken from his desk.

I leafed through the cash book. 'Have you seen this before?'

'Possibly. I don't really know. I didn't get involved in the business much.' Her breath was warm on my cheek when she spoke. She was standing very close, looking down at the book with me.

Scattered amongst the entries were the addresses of residential properties. 'Did he buy these places?' I asked.

'Probably. A couple of years ago he was

126

acquiring largish run-down houses in reasonable areas, refurbishing them or converting them into luxury flats, and then selling them on. He never kept any, because he was always wanting cash to speculate with.'

'Where did your husband have his yard?'

'Yard?' She sounded puzzled.

'Where he kept his materials and lorries and such like.'

She smiled. 'He didn't do business like that, Mr Lomax. He was what you'd call entrepreneurial. He used to find a client or some run-down property, hire an architect to draw plans, then use subcontractors to do the actual work. He never employed men direct.'

'Did he have any offices in Barfield?'

She laughed. 'He had a plate saying 'Registered Office of Rex Saunders Enterprises Limited' fixed on the gazebo. A solicitor told him it satisfied the Companies Act.'

'Gazebo?'

'The summer house in the corner of the garden. It wasn't really a summer house. It was the top of an ornamental clock tower Rex salvaged from a building that was demolished. At ground level it's surprisingly large. He had French windows fitted and it was all painted white. It's quite pretty in an ornate kind of way. Rex used to think it was a great joke: the registered office in a gazebo, I mean. He was like that.' Her voice had become shaky. Talking about her husband and the gazebo thing seemed to be tearing her apart.

'Have you any idea why anyone would want to kill your husband, Mrs Saunders?' I tried to make my voice gentle.

Her eyes were filling up and her tiny chin was trembling. She shook her head. 'Only the money he owed. It could only have been that.'

'Creditors would want him alive so they could get it back. They'd only kill if they were certain they'd no chance of making a recovery.' I studied the almost too perfect face for a while. It only revealed how bewildered and scared she was, nothing more. Presently I said, 'You told me he might be having an affair. What made you suspect that?'

'He'd hired you to spy on me and I suppose I was feeling hurt. And he'd been so remote and distant; we hadn't had a . . . a married life for months.' She blushed crimson at that. 'When a husband completely loses interest, it's only natural for a wife to suspect there's another woman.'

She gazed at me across the honey-coloured dining-table. After a while she said softly, 'I'm sure in Rex's case it was worry. Or me. Looking back, I realize I neglected him a little. I just indulged myself, spending the money he made. Perhaps my neglect and his worries had made him start suspecting me. Oh God, I . . . '

She was letting it all go now. The tears were coursing down her cheeks and she was snuffling back the mucus. I helped her to a chintzy sofa. I didn't have a handkerchief — I seldom do — so I went into the kitchen and got a towel.

I sat close and put my arm around her shoulders. She felt hot and feverish through the silky material of her suit. After a while, the tension seemed to leave her body. She relaxed into me and the sobbing subsided.

'I'm sorry, Mr Lomax. Rex, the police, I just . . . '

'Don't worry about the police, Mrs Saunders. They won't be troubling you any more.'

★   ★   ★

The dashboard clock was showing a little after five when I parked on the concrete hardstanding at the side of my own dilapidated little bungalow. I picked up Saunders's papers, did some ritual wrestling with the sticking front door and stepped inside. When I reached the phone in the hall,

I dialled Maslow's number.

'Nine-four-six-three-seven, Mr Maslow's residence.' Her voice was breathless, as if she'd sprinted to answer the phone. Somehow her broad Yorkshire accent didn't fit the mental picture I had of her.

'I figured I might come over and read you that bedtime story, Gloriana, when you've finished handing out the After Eights.'

She giggled. 'Mr Maslow doesn't eat After Eights. Anyway, I'm a big girl now. I don't need bedtime stories.'

'Then maybe I could help blow out your night-light?'

'Honey, ten minutes up there with me and you won't have enough breath left to blow out a night-light.' She was laughing now. I could hear the low, body-shaking sound of it echoing around Maslow's massive entrance hall.

'How's Fido?' I was changing the subject, chickening out.

'Fido?'

'The dog.'

'It's dead. Started foaming at the mouth. Mr Maslow told Kelly to take one of the shotguns and put it down.'

'I can't say I'm sorry.'

'Me neither. It scared me just knowing it was across the yard.'

130

'Could you put me through to Mr Maslow, Gloriana?'

'He hates to be disturbed.'

'Just tell him it's me. It'll be OK.'

I heard a clicking, a brief silence, then Maslow barked, 'Mr Lomax?' down the line.

I told him it was.

'Tracked the cash down already, old boy?'

'Not yet, Mr Maslow. I'm phoning because I want you to do something for me.'

He made a disappointed noise, then said warily, 'What is it?'

'The police: you said you'd keep them off my back. I want you to stop them pestering Saunders's widow, too.'

'There's a limit to how many strings I can pull, old boy.'

'She didn't kill her husband, and the cops must know it. I need her accessible and as calm as we can get her, if I'm going to find out what old Rex did with the cash.'

'Very well,' he said irritably. 'I'll see what I can do. But you'd better get on with the job. Tulley came over after you'd gone. I told him I was putting out feelers and managed to persuade him to leave it alone for a few days. He's getting very impatient, though.'

'I'll do my best, Mr Maslow, but I'll need more than a few days.'

'You'll have to do a damned sight better

131

than that. I can only hold Tulley off for so long, and then it'll be God help you and the widow when he comes looking for the cash.' His clipped voice was cold and hard. There was more than a hint of menace in it, too.

'Just get the police off Mona Saunders's back. I'll take care of the rest.'

'Mr Lomax?' he said quickly, as if he was afraid I was going to ring off.

'Yeah?'

'The first half-million you find is mine. Tulley can have what you come across after that.'

I heard a click, then the buzzing of a disconnected line, and I cradled the receiver.

Still clutching the papers, I padded through to the kitchen, peered inside the fridge, feasted my eyes on an urgent defrosting job, some old food wrappers and the festering remains of a pork pie. I slammed the door, ignored the foodsmeared plates in the sink and wandered into the living room.

I turned up the gas fire, settled myself in a chair and worked my way down a bottle of Scotch while I leafed through Saunders's cash book. He seemed to have been a shrewd operator: fast turnover, letting other guys do the work and take most of the risks while he took the profits. Maslow had been right. Judging by the dates and the profit mark-ups,

Saunders certainly knew how to turn a pound into a tenner fast.

I kept flicking back to a property deal dated about two years earlier and suddenly realized what was bugging me. The purchase price was entered, and the cost of conversion into three flats, but he'd only penned in the sale proceeds from two units. With his track record it seemed unlikely he'd missed an entry or been unable to sell the third flat. Mona had just told me he always sold, never leased. There's always the exception that proves the rule, but I'd so little to go on, anything remotely out of the ordinary was worth noting.

I took a peep inside the diary. It was that year's and seemed to have been used for appointments: just initials and times, no details of the nature of the business. One set of initials, J.T., figured once, sometimes twice a week, and always on a Thursday afternoon, with the other times at random.

I began to trawl through the rest of the papers, but too much heat in a small room, too much whisky on an empty stomach, and too much thinking, were ganging-up on me. I switched off the gas fire and the lights, then headed for the bedroom.

After making a pretence of putting my suit on a hanger, I burrowed between the clammy sheets of an unmade bed, trying hard to forget what holding Melody had felt like; how hot and feverish Mona Saunders had been when I'd tried to comfort her that afternoon.

11

We motored through the outer limits of the town, past grubby shops, advertisement hoardings and sleazy tenements. Mona Saunders's fragrance was filling the car; her endless legs were stretched out beside me. She was wearing a short-sleeved yellow cotton dress. I was driving slowly, in no hurry for the journey to end.

I risked a glance at her. Sunglasses in thin gold frames hid her eyes, like shutters on rooms full of unhappy memories and frightening dreams. When she looked at me, her lips parted in a smile. She seemed to be enjoying a brief respite from sadness. Maybe it was because the cops had phoned her and said they wouldn't be taking her in for more questioning. One joy can sometimes banish a lot of grief: for a while, anyway.

'Thanks for coming with me to the house, Mr Lomax. I know it's silly of me, but I'm afraid to go there alone. I won't keep you waiting long. I only want to collect a few personal things.'

I smiled at her to let her know it was OK. The way she looked, the sound of her voice, the clean-perfumed smell of her body; it was a pleasure doing her the favour.

We left down-town Barfield behind and took the road up through sprawling suburbs where decaying Edwardian villas gave way to the smart new houses of the latest generation of high-achievers. And then there were fields, misty and golden in the September morning sunlight.

I turned into the narrow lane that led to Ravenstone House. The sun was shining into my eyes now. I pulled down the visor, glanced at her and asked, 'What did your husband do on Thursday afternoons, Mrs Saunders?'

She gave me a puzzled look, then shrugged and said, 'Worked, swam, pottered about around the house. Never any one particular thing. His time wasn't organized in that way.'

'He didn't have a regular appointment, or a regular caller?'

'I don't think so,' she said.

'The initials J.T., do they mean anything to you?'

She frowned. 'No, nothing.'

'And your husband hadn't been out of the country recently?'

'I don't think he could have been. He was never away from the house long enough: a morning and afternoon, an afternoon and evening. Never longer than that.'

'Would you know if he had a safe deposit box?'

'I'm pretty sure he'd tell me something like that. I dealt with the joint bank account. I suppose I spent most of the money in it. Rex was very shrewd, Mr Lomax. He used his money to make more and managed to get away with paying very little tax. He'd an aversion to banks. The joint account hadn't much more than household expenses and my allowance in it. I'll check if you like, though. When we get to the house, I'll phone the bank.'

I eased the car into the drive, then cruised over the fancy paving bricks and parked in front of the house. I used one of the keys on the bunch she'd given me to let us in. When she stepped inside, she gazed around the high space with its first-floor gallery, hugged herself, and shivered. Her lips started trembling.

'I'm glad you came, Mr Lomax. I used to love this house, but now its shadows scare me.'

'There's some tools and other gear behind the fireplace, and the back door's wedged shut with a chair,' I said.

She took the sunglasses off and looked at me.

'I disturbed a burglar when I came to get

the papers for you. He left his kit behind.'

'A burglar!' She shivered again. That little bit of news had really set her nerves jangling.

We wandered through the huge lounge. The tools were still there beside the safe. When we went into the kitchen, a chair still wedged the outer door shut.

We made our way back to the hall. She began to climb the stairs, then stopped and looked down at me with those scared, bewildered eyes. 'What am I going to do? Dear God, what am I going to do?'

I met her gaze for a moment, then said gently, 'Your husband was in a lot of trouble, Mrs Saunders. He'd upset some seriously violent people. For both our sakes, I've got to find the money fast. If you think of anything that might help, anything at all, you've got to tell me.'

She nodded dumbly.

'Would you mind if I left you for half an hour?' I asked.

Her body tensed. 'Can't you wait with me?' Her voice sounded panicky and reproachful.

'I just want to check something. I won't be far away.'

'But . . . '

'I'll try and make it twenty minutes.' I gave her a reassuring smile.

'Oh, very well,' she said, in a petulant little

138

voice. 'But come and look over the upstairs rooms with me before you go.'

★　★　★

The canine chorus was audible long before I reached the end of the track and jolted across the rutted yard. On my left was the rear of a drab red-brick farmhouse with a slate roof; up ahead, a low brick building blocked the view across the fields; on my right, an open barn was stacked with bales of straw and the usual clutter of farm machinery.

I cut the motor. Even through the closed windows of the car, the barking was loud and frenzied. I climbed out, strolled over to the house and knocked on a heavy boarded door, then studied peeling paint and sagging gutters, listening to the frenzied barking of the dogs. There was no answer. When I stepped back, a movement behind a first-floor window caught my eye. There was someone there all right, half-hidden by a net curtain, features made colourless and indistinct by the reflection of clouds and sky off the glass. It was the face of a woman. When I smiled up at her, the net curtain fell back, concealing her again.

'And what would you be wanting?'

I spun round. A heavily built guy was

standing by the car, hostility in his eyes and in the set of his body. His features were deeply lined and weather-beaten; thick, wet lips were ringed by a two-day growth of dark stubble. He was trying hard to hide a receding hairline by combing forward the thinning remnants of his grey hair. He wore a military-style khaki turtleneck sweater with leather elbow and shoulder patches, brown corduroys, and muddy wellington boots. A large-bore shotgun lay, breach open, in the crook of his arm.

'Pit bulls,' I said. 'I hear you breed pit bulls.'

He just stared at me.

I strolled over to him, got my face close to his. 'I'm interested in pit bulls,' I repeated.

'Who told you I breed pit bulls?' His voice was gravelly and deep; the sort of voice you'd get from drinking drain-cleaner.

'Maslow,' I said. 'Frederick Maslow.'

His body relaxed a little when I said that, and interest began to dilute the hostility in his eyes, but he didn't speak.

'Maybe you could show me some?'

'Interested in buying, or are you just wasting my time? I don't like smartarse time-wasters.'

'Depends what you've got. I'm looking for a real red-blooded fighting-dog, not some powder-puff pooch.'

'Listen, mister, my dogs are big, bad and deadly. Bred to fight and kill. Any that don't come up to the mark get fed to the rest.'

He suddenly realized I'd been goading him. His fleshy mouth curved into a grin, exposing teeth that were small and wide-spaced. The whole effect was crafty and sly, like the village idiot trying to sell a tourist the clock tower.

I grinned back.

He turned, gestured for me to follow, began taking big, bandy-legged strides across the rutted yard towards the building up ahead.

Inside, the racket was deafening. He closed and bolted the door, sealing it in, then yelled out names and abuse until the barking subsided. He led me down a row of cages erected in what had once been pig-pens. The dogs were black as night; mostly unscarred versions of the animal I'd seen going berserk at Maslow's place.

I stopped beside the biggest, most vicious looking beast in the pack and said, 'How much?'

'Jet's not for sale.'

'That's the one I want,' I insisted.

'Pick another, he's not for sale.'

'I'll give you three thousand.'

He laughed. 'You've got to be kidding. Anyway, he's sold. Maslow phoned first thing and bought her.' He pointed at the dog in the next cage. 'You can have Bruce for three and a half. Bit more training, say another couple of months, and he'll be the pick of the bunch.'

'I'd prefer the one you call Jet, but I'll think about it.'

I looked down at straw and droppings and urine-soaked concrete, the stainless steel water-bowls, the nearly wild killing machines with their glittering beetle-black eyes. Puppies were sucking at a bitch in the end pen. The bitch was snarling at me through bared teeth. I grinned at her owner, then turned and headed for the door. He followed me through.

'I'll think it over and give you a ring,' I said. 'What's your number?'

He recited some digits.

'And it's . . . ?'

'Hawkins,' he offered. Then he asked, 'How do you know Fred Maslow?'

'Meat business,' I said.

'Local, are you?'

'No, Ramford City.'

We strolled across the yard and I tried to sound casual as I said, 'That fancy modern house back there on the lane, isn't it the place where some guy was murdered?'

He eyed me warily. 'Yeah,' he said. 'What of it?'

'Just curious. Read about it in the paper. Recognized the house from the picture.'

'Don't remember seeing a picture of the house in the paper.'

'*Ramford Echo* printed one,' I assured him blithely. I'd no idea what the papers had said about it all.

A truck clattered into the yard. There was some noisy gear-changing, then it reversed towards us. A muscular arm held the cab door slightly open; a tanned face peered out. He had plenty of black hair, and the bushy black moustache was still curling around his mouth like a dying rodent. It was the amateur box-man I'd surprised at the Saunders' place; one of Andrew Tulley's sons.

The truck juddered to a stop with its tail-board close to the dog-house door. He sprang out and strutted towards us with a kind of assertive animal vigour. He looked taller and younger than he had in the torchlight.

He grinned at Hawkins and gave me a curt nod. His faded jeans were like a coarse second skin. The sleeves of his yellow check shirt were rolled up above the elbow. It was unbuttoned at the neck, revealing some more of the tan and the beginnings of a pelt of frizzy black hair.

I turned towards Hawkins. 'Thanks for showing me the dogs. Is there a pit around here where I could see some action, have a wager maybe?'

'Why didn't you ask Frank Maslow?' Hawkins gave Tulley a narrow-eyed look.

'Didn't think to. I was more concerned with finding a dog.'

'When you've bought a dog, we'll help you arrange a roll,' Hawkins said.

I tried to look genial, nodded a goodbye, and when I strode off down the side of the truck, I could feel their eyes on me. As I moved out to avoid the open door of the cab, I glanced inside. A bunch of keys was hanging from the ignition switch on the steering column. For some reason I couldn't put my finger on, it held my gaze and I had to jerk my shoulder back to avoid slamming it into the edge of the door.

Reaching the car, I glanced towards the house and saw the woman at the upstairs window again. From where I was standing now there was no reflection of sunlight on the glass to ghost my view of her. I guessed she'd be around forty. She was a few pounds overweight and her features had a pleasant, homely softness. She was looking intently at the two men by the tail-board of the truck. She didn't spare me a glance. Her hair had a reddish tinge to it, and around her right eye and all down that side of her face was a patch of darkness. Scar, bruise, birthmark: I couldn't tell.

I pulled open the door of the car, began to climb inside.

'You sure you're not local?' Tulley yelled across the yard.

I slammed the door, started the engine and wound down the window. 'Ramford City,' I yelled back.

'Reckon I've seen you around.'

'Probably. I come to Barfield a lot.'

'What did you say your name was?'

I revved the engine, kept my voice just below the level of the din, and bawled, 'Flop House Ferdie.' I gave them a great big smile, a friendly wave, let out the clutch and jolted off up the lane.

★ ★ ★

Mona Saunders was waiting, tense and agitated, in the open doorway of Ravenstone House.

'You've been ages,' she said accusingly. 'Murderers, burglars; you know I'm scared to death of the place, but you still left me

145

alone here all this time.'

I told her I was sorry without sounding it, and asked her to get into the car.

'The cases are in the hall,' she snapped. She was glaring at me with those huge dark eyes, letting me know what a bad boy I'd been. She flashed me a smile that was like a slap on the wrist, then strutted over to the Jaguar.

I wanted to be away before Tulley came back down the lane in his truck and saw me at the house, or with Mona Saunders in the car; so I begrudged the few minutes it took me to load the pile of matching red leather suitcases, hat boxes, make-up cases and other paraphernalia into the back and boot of the Jaguar.

When we were well down the Barfield Road, with nothing in the rear view mirror, I relaxed a little. She turned the sunglasses on me, smiled a proper smile and said, 'I'm sorry I was so rude back there, Mr Lomax. I was terribly scared. Where on earth did you get to?'

'The farm down the lane. Hawkins's place.'

She shuddered. 'He breeds those awful dogs. Sometimes you can hear them howling and barking at night. Rex used to go there. I went with him once. I was nearly sick. Do you know how they train the brutes?'

I said I didn't.

'They starve them for a couple of days, then slash a kitten or a weakling puppy with a razor to make it bleed, and put it in the cage for them to tear to pieces. Rex told me it was to make the dogs associate food and drink with blood and killing.'

I didn't say anything. She sat there, angry and distraught, her body tense. After a while she said bitterly, 'Men like that make me sick. And they're the type who despise sweet sensitive people like Vivian Delmar. He wouldn't dream of doing things like that.'

We completed the journey in silence. I carried the car-load of luggage up on to the access deck and into her friend's flat.

'Your husband's first wife, is she still around?' I was standing on the access deck; she was just inside the narrow hall.

'I can't think how his first wife can possibly interest you,' she said sharply.

'Everything to do with your husband interests me, Mrs Saunders.'

She gave me a disapproving look. 'Come back in. I'll see if I can find her address for you.'

We went back into the sitting-room. Mona flopped down on the sofa, pulled her handbag on to her lap, clicked it open and began to rummage around. The full skirt of her yellow dress had ridden up and her hair was falling around her face. I sat on one of the spindly dining-chairs, taking in the view. When my pulse rate had crept beyond the danger level, I dragged my eyes away and studied the travel posters decorating the walls.

After what seemed like a great deal of searching, she unfolded a letter and read me the address that headed it. I noted it down.

'I'm sorry I don't have a telephone number.'

'No worries. I can get it from the address. Did you ever meet her?'

'No.' She said that hastily and with a little shudder. 'Rex had left her long before we met. She had a very good job in Ramford. About a year ago, Rex got a letter from her solicitor saying she was going to sue for maintenance. Apparently she'd been made redundant and was having to sell the house. Rex didn't haggle or go to court. I wouldn't have wanted him to. I suppose I still felt guilty about Rex and me. He just settled on a figure, and a cheque goes every month.'

We looked at one another for a few moments; then she seemed to remember something. 'Oh, by the way, I phoned the bank. Rex didn't have a safe deposit box.'

'Thanks,' I said.

Her face was starting to crumple again, and

her eyes were too bright. 'Will you be going to see Rex's first wife?'

'Yeah,' I said. 'I'm going to look her up.'

'Tell her . . . Tell her I'll contact her about the funeral arrangements when the police release the body to me.'

Tears began to bucket down and she choked out a couple of hefty sobs. When I made to go over to her, she tugged her dress down and snapped, 'It's bad enough feeling guilty about having neglected Rex, without all this remorse over his first wife.'

'You said he'd left her before you met.'

'I'm a lapsed Catholic, Mr Lomax. We're talking about good old-fashioned guilt here. Something you'd find hard to understand.'

I looked down at her, watching her snuffle into a tiny little handkerchief. The lousy business I was in, the things I had to do to sort out the sordid problems people like her got themselves into: I could have given her lessons in guilt.

I began to say something soothing, but she just cut across me, snapped out between sobs, 'I'd like you to go now, Mr Lomax. I want to be left alone.'

12

I collected the mail from the box behind my slot, climbed up to the office, slid behind the desk and got to work with a paper-knife. A car tax renewal notice, a subpoena to give evidence in a fraud case; no cheques, no fan mail. I dumped the envelopes in the bin, grabbed the phone and dialled Maslow's number.

A Scottish-sounding guy answered. Maybe it was the one who'd helped collect me the day before. I asked for Maslow and the line went clickety-click. I imagined that Gloriana must be serving up lunch. Nothing too heavy: a little veal casseroled in wine, a few sautéd potatoes, some sprigs of broccoli . . .

'Lomax, old chap. You've got news for me at last.' Relief, expectancy, hope; they all mingled in that clipped, ultra-refined voice of his.

'Not yet, Mr Maslow. I just wanted to let you know I looked over Hawkins's place this morning; told him I was interested in buying a dog. I said I came from Ramford City, knew you through the meat business, and you'd recommended him. Back me up if he mentions it.'

'Did you have to, dammit?'

'Got to check out everything, Mr Maslow. Saunders was interested in pit bulls and he used to visit the place, so I thought I'd look it over. Some guy I think was Hawkins's partner was there.'

'Swarthy, arrogant young beggar; black moustache, black hair?'

'That's right.'

'Jack Tulley . . . And he saw you?'

'Sure he saw me.'

'Be careful, Lomax. If they ever find out who you are, for heaven's sake don't let them know you're working for me.' There was a shaky undercurrent of fear in his voice now.

I said I wouldn't.

'Tulley's been pestering me again this morning. The blighter's running out of patience. He's beginning to suspect me. He won't wait much longer; another day at the most and he'll come looking for his cash. Heaven knows what the crazy beggar will do if he doesn't find it quick.'

I replaced the receiver, scowled down at the doodles on the blotter. A spider scurried out, took a peek at me, then legged it for cover down a narrow canyon between the heaps of papers.

151

The phone shrilled. I snatched it up, grunted my name and number.

'You're a crafty, conniving swine, Lomax.'

'Everybody's paying me compliments. Which silver-tongued flatterer is talking to me now?'

'Sloane, Chief Inspector Sloane. I've been in the force thirty years, but nobody's ever managed to pull my strings before.'

'Strings?'

'You know what I mean. Having me dragged off your back and told to go easy on Mona Saunders.'

'You must be crazy. How could I interfere with the Old Bill? I don't even know who to complain to to get my dustbin emptied.'

'Spare me the pathetic quips, Lomax. You're not half as smart as you think you are. You might have got me and Mace off your back, but something evil's brewing up for you and the widow. Don't expect us to come running when you squeal. You're on your own.'

'Tell me something new next time,' I growled, then slammed the receiver down.

I began to turn the whole lousy mess over in my mind, but no leads, no facts and an IQ not much bigger than my collarsize stopped me getting very far. Some smart operator who had an aversion to banks and the tax-man

152

had borrowed a million from two citizens who liked the tax-man even less. And Saunders hadn't spent a penny on the scheme he'd collected the cash for. Maybe something had gone adrift with the time-share flats thing and he'd shied off. Then again, he might have conned the cash out of them for some short-term speculation, but that didn't seem like Saunders's style, and he'd have had plenty of explaining to do when the money they'd lent him didn't realize a profit. Always assuming, of course, that foxy old Rex had intended to stick around and do some explaining. But then, with ravishing Mona to share his dream home and all his other worldly goods, I figured he'd have stuck around.

I heard crockery rattle, the patter of high heels, then Melody breezed in with the lunchtime tray.

'My, we are looking jaded.'

'It's this lousy business,' I moaned. 'Too little of it, and what there is always seems to be the wrong kind. And on the odd occasion you actually get paid, there's hardly enough left after expenses to buy yourself a secondhand hairpiece.'

She reached over and set the tray down on the blotter.

'I got you a chicken salad, that OK?'

'Thanks, that's fine.' I gazed up at her. She was dressed all in black and she'd pinned the blonde curls on top of her head. The neckline of the sweater was plunging lower than the pound, and the shapes beneath were defying gravity in a spectacular kind of way. I didn't even try to hide my total fascination with it all. She began to ladle sugar into the coffee.

'Where did you get to yesterday? I had one of the girls fetch you a curry in.'

'I got tied up with the Saunders business.'

I didn't tell her about the intimate little meal with Mona. No use kissing my lunchtime creature comforts goodbye in a moment of meaningless honesty.

'You're still haunting her dreams, then?'

'Huh?' I swallowed a mouthful of chicken.

'Mona Saunders: haunting her dreams.'

'Hardly. She's into sweet, sensitive, limp-wristed guys. She told me she's tired of big physical types with their animal appetites.'

Melody was smiling at me now and her big blue eyes were twinkling. 'Rebuffed you, has she?'

'She's not had to. I never mix business with pleasure.'

Melody gave me a disbelieving look. 'It was probably her way of telling you how much her husband had upset her. If she was really attracted to the sweet sensitive type, she'd

154

have married one.'

'And how do you know all this?'

'I am a woman, too, you know.'

I managed to drag my eyes off the sweater, grinned up at her and said, 'I had noticed.'

She gave me one of her reproachful little sighs. 'I think I'm beginning to see what Mona Saunders means about animal appetites. You eat like a starving timber-wolf, and if you go on staring at every woman you meet like that, they'll take you away and plug you into the mains.'

'I don't.'

'Don't what?'

'Stare at every woman that way. Only a special few.'

She struggled to hide the smile. 'One of a few, am I? Anyway, I'm sure you won't have any problems with Mona. She'll not be able to resist the Lomax charm for long.'

'You didn't find it difficult.'

She eyed me steadily for a moment, her arms folded beneath her breasts. Then she slowly came round to my side of the desk and said, 'I'd hoped we could both forget that, Paul.'

'That bad, was it?'

'You know what I mean.' She was giving me an embarrassed little smile now.

I frowned. 'No, I can't say that I do. Great

meal, perfect evening; I didn't get that cup of coffee you promised, but if Saunders had kept his nose out of things I might have.'

'I was glad he phoned. I don't like to think where things would have ended if he'd not.'

'I can't think about anything else.'

I was looking up at her. She was standing very close. I let the chair swing a little until our legs touched. She didn't move away, but spots of colour began to glow on her cheeks. I couldn't recall seeing her this embarrassed before. She was the very last person I'd want to make uncomfortable, but I couldn't let this one rest.

'Please, Paul. Don't look at me like that. Don't go all serious on me. The teasing, the silly little jokes; we both do it to keep the bogeymen at bay, don't we? We're two of a kind. If we stop the banter, get all serious, the memories will start flooding in. I don't know about you, but I don't think I could cope. I've got too many lousy memories.'

Suddenly she smiled. She was switching back into bright-and-breezy mode. 'So, Paul, the goodnight kiss is something else we ought to try and forget, because it's not going to happen again.'

She began to head for the door, her neat little posterior swaying in an electrifyingly elemental way that called for serious study. I consider myself a leading world authority on posterior-sway in the human female.

'I didn't think it was a goodnight kiss,' I called after her. 'I thought it was an utterly unforgettable prelude to . . . '

She paused in the doorway and looked back. 'You're not helping me with this, Paul. And there's mayonnaise all over your chin and down the front of that nice new tie.'

I listened to her tap-tapping over the linoleum in the reception-room, trying to hold on to the vision of that swaying posterior.

★   ★   ★

The small market town where Saunders's first wife lived was about ten miles east of Barfield. When I crossed the ring road, heading out, I realized the flat shown in his cash book as unsold was close by. I decided to kill two birds with one stone and check it over. I made a left and began to motor along an avenue of big Victorian terraced houses. Some had been converted into offices and dental surgeries, the rest carved up into flats, but behind the tall plane trees that lined the roadway nestled an atmosphere of quiet respectability; fresh paint and sparkling glass, a refusal to succumb to neglect and decay.

I cruised on well past the house, parked in a vacant slot, then strolled back along the opposite side of the street. It was quiet and almost deserted, just as a street in that part of town should be at 2.30 on a September weekday afternoon.

There were no signs of movement behind the ground and first-floor windows of number 56. From where I was standing, the second floor windows were hidden by the tired, end of season foliage of a roadside tree. I ambled over, climbed the half-dozen steps that rose off the pavement to a big entrance door which had a glass panel with an intricate floral design etched into it. Inside the shallow porch were three bell-pushes fixed alongside small brass frames that held name-cards. I vaguely remembered the names for the first and second-floor flats from Saunders's cash book. The name given for the ground-floor flat wasn't familiar. I punched the bell, waited, then punched it some more. No one answered. I tried the door. It was locked.

The fancy brass knob was still shiny and new-looking. At its centre was a slot for a key. I took out the bunch Mona Saunders had given me and selected one that had a long blade and serrations down both edges, like a car ignition key, only longer. It slid into the aperture in the knob, turned smoothly, and I was stepping through on to tiny coloured tiles.

I closed the door, listened for sounds, heard nothing. On my left was a letter-rack with three pigeonholes. Straight ahead, past a carpeted flight of stairs, sunlight was pouring through the reeded glass panel of a door that probably led out to the back. On my right was the doorway of the ground-floor flat.

I knocked, just in case the bell had failed to rouse the occupiers, but kept it gentle enough to avoid interesting anyone who might be upstairs. There was still no answer.

The flat door was secured by an ordinary cylinder lock. I worked my way through likely looking keys and presently found one that turned. I heard the sneck click, then moved on into a narrow inner lobby.

I did a quick reconnoitre. There was a large sitting-room at the front, and a decent-sized bedroom, smallish bathroom and tiny kitchen at the rear. Carpets were plain, deep and wall-to-wall; decorations tasteful and subdued; furnishings sparse, but good-quality. There was a small portable television in the sitting-room, a cheap radio in the kitchen and a fancy telephone beside the bed. There were no clothes in the fitted wardrobes, nothing in the dressing-table drawers; no books, magazines or ornaments; and no food in the kitchen. A small airing-cupboard near the bathroom was crammed with clean towels, sheets and blankets. I put my hand on the pipework at the top of the cylinder. It was hot.

A Venetian blind screened the bedroom window. I pressed down one of the slats and peered out over the sunlit rear yard. The whole area had been surfaced with tarmac, and an opening in the high back wall gave on to a rear access road.

I heard a faint clatter and the slam of a door, then footsteps came padding down the narrow passage that led to the bedroom. I glanced around. Nothing taller than a young snake could have wriggled under the divan bed. The only hiding-place was the fitted wardrobe. Like an actor in a third-rate farce, I climbed inside, pulled the louvred doors shut behind me and grabbed at a bunch of coathangers to stop them rattling on the rail. I heard someone enter the bedroom, the crackle of paper bags, the muffled thuds of feet walking over thick carpet.

One of the wardrobe doors began to swing open. I held my breath, managed to hook a finger over a louvre and stop it moving further.

She was visible now, through the narrow opening between the doors. She dropped paper bags beside the dressing table and peeled off a shabby raincoat to reveal a cotton dress that had had all of the colour and life washed and ironed out of it. She wasn't wearing any stockings. Her flat-heeled shoes were scuffed and tired looking.

She unbuttoned the dress and stepped out of it, then kicked off the shoes. Soft, creamy flesh seemed to billow above the lacy bodice of her black silk slip, and its thin straps were cutting into her plump shoulders. She picked up one of the dress-shop bags and moved around the bed, out of my field of view. When she reappeared, she was wearing fluffy, high-heeled bedroom slippers and modelling a floor-trailing black négligé. She did some hand-on-hip posing in front of the mirror, then took a lipstick from her handbag and carefully gave her big, soft-looking mouth the works. She rummaged in her bag again, found a comb, teased reddish-brown curls into place, then stepped back to check the effect.

She'd moved out of view, but I could see her reflection in the mirror. She was pouting her lips, tilting her chin to tighten up the skin around her throat. It was then that I recognized those homely, still-attractive features, which were marred by the fading remnants of a massive bruise. It was the

161

woman I'd seen gazing out of the window at Hawkins's farm.

She did some more of the Mae West style hip thrusting, exchanged a secret little smile with her reflection, then gathered up the dress and shoes and raincoat and headed for the wardrobe. I took a deep breath, tensed myself, got ready to leap out, dash over the bed and away before she could get a good look at me. I gripped the louvres of the door that was concealing me, and held on tight. The other door swung open. I watched a small hand dart inside, grab a hanger and disappear.

The telephone began its frantic cheep-cheeping. Her footsteps receded around the bed and there was a clatter as she picked up the receiver.

When she said, 'Hello,' her voice was wary and apprehensive, as if she didn't want to answer the call. And then she laughed and said, 'Oh, hello, love. It's you. I wondered who on earth it could be . . . ' She listened for a while, then said, 'I don't understand, love. What do you mean you can't make it?'

I'd seen her in her underwear, but it was the first time I'd heard her speak. Her voice was like her body: warm, soft and mature, with enough of a Yorkshire accent in it to make it homely, but not so much that it became coarse.

I could hear her deep breathing, the metallic twittering of a voice at the other end of the line, the creak of bedsprings as she sat down.

'But I've got to see you. I don't understand why you won't come. It's safe here. Nobody knows about it; nobody *could* know, all the care we've taken.' She was pleading with the party at the other end of the line. 'You don't know what I've been through. He was like a raving lunatic. An animal wouldn't have done the things he did to me. I'm covered in bruises. I've got to . . . '

She stopped talking, did some more heavy breathing while she listened to the voice at the other end of the line.

Presently she said, 'He's never seen us together, and no one could have told him because no one knows. We've been so damned careful, it hurts.'

She paused again. In the silence, I could hear the faint sound of the caller's voice, but couldn't make out the words.

'I didn't tell him, love,' she said. 'He worked it out for himself. He looked in my bag for some fags and saw the underwear I wore last time, then he really started searching and found the suspender-belts and stockings and all the other things I'd hidden in a drawer. I've never worn clothes like that for him. It'd be like throwing pearls before swine. He's worse than those dogs he breeds. And he's mean and cunning, but he knew something must be going on. He's not that stupid, love. He just put two and two together . . . '

There was more of the faint twittering.

'That's why I've got to see you. I've got to talk to somebody about it. I was in such a mess after he'd hit me, I didn't think to phone and warn him, and you can't imagine what it's been like having that on my conscience.' And then her voice became softer and more seductive as she went on, 'I'm wearing something special. That present you gave me; I used it to buy something you'll really like. You can kiss my bruises better, all of them, kiss them till they go away. We can do what we did last time,' she gave a throaty chuckle, 'you know, when you . . . '

I caught the metallic twittering, louder this time, and sensed he was having another go at giving her the brush-off. She was getting the message. She didn't let him go on long before she blurted out, 'You said you loved me, but when I really need you you don't even want to know! I feel used and cheap.' Her voice was plaintive now, drenched with bitterness

164

and anger; the voice of a woman who'd begun to realize she'd been casting her cultured pearls before an even bigger swine than the one she had at home. 'You pig,' she sobbed. 'You lousy pig. If you were a real man, you'd have come and taken me away after what he did to me. I wish I'd told him it *was* you now. I loved you so much, I even told that lie for you. What do you think — '

I guessed Mr Wonderful had hung up. The sound of her breathing grew louder and louder until it was a raucous groaning. Then she crashed down the receiver, wailed, 'Bastard!' and burst into a fit of hysterical sobbing.

My neck ached from being bent under the low shelf, my right leg had gone to sleep, I needed the toilet with a burning desperation, but I had to go on standing there, listening to her sob out her anger and grief. After what seemed like an eternity, the bedsprings creaked and she began to move around the room again.

Circulation had stopped long ago. I couldn't tense muscles I could no longer feel. If she yanked open the door this time, I knew I'd just drop in a heap on the carpet.

She approached the wardrobe. I could hear her snuffling and sobbing on the other side of the louvres as she gathered up her things, then she moved in and out of my narrow field of view as she dressed. I saw her peering into the mirror. Her face was sore and blotchy-looking now, as well as bruised. She'd discarded the voluptuous *femme fatale* personality with the négligé: re-clothed herself in the dowdy reality of the overweight housewife when she'd put the faded dress and raincoat back on. She took a handkerchief from her pocket and stared tearfully into the mirror while she wiped her lips clean of lipstick. Then she struggled into her shoes, grabbed her handbag and disappeared from view.

I heard three doors slam, then tottered, stiff, aching, bladder bursting, from the wardrobe.

13

I caught the fragrance as I rounded the top of the stairs and walked across the landing: stale aftershave, male sweat and cigarette smoke.

The full force hit me when I pushed open the office door and stepped into the fug. The cause was lounging on red plastic chairs, feet up on the magazine table. Five causes: a grey-haired father and four black-haired sons. Swarthy, muscular; their good suits spoiled by creases and open-necked shirts with no ties. The family resemblance was striking. The Tulleys were paying me a social call.

They were silent. I guess they'd heard me thumping up the stairs, stopped talking and waited. They were watching me with arrogant, curious eyes.

I looked from one lean swarthy face to the next until the guy I'd met at Hawkins's farm said, 'Yeah, that's him all right.'

I crossed my arms, leant back against the door and worked my features into an affable expression. It wasn't easy.

'You're Lomax, the private investigator?' asked the one I'd taken to be the father.

'That's what's written all over the door,' I said.

'Don't get smart, or I'll really lose my patience,' he grated.

He pushed himself out of the chair and lumbered over. He was tall, as tall as me, maybe six-one or two. Age and too much weight had slowed him down, but that's all it had done. When he shoved his face up close to mine, I caught the smell of beer and cigarette smoke on his breath. His left eyelid drooped over a glass eye that was holding me in a fixed stare. His good eye was red and bloodshot, flickering restlessly over my features, struggling to make up for its useless brother. A wet, fleshy bottom lip sagged under its own weight. It made him look sullen and stupid. I figured the last thing he was was stupid.

'What were you snooping around Hawkins's farm for?' His voice was throaty and rough; a ragged, heavy smoker's voice.

'Sporting dogs,' I said. 'Pit bulls. I'm interested.'

'Liar.' He punched me on the shoulder. 'That crafty old devil Maslow's hired you, hasn't he?'

'Maslow? I don't know any Maslow.' I stared into his good eye.

'He knows who Maslow is.' The son I'd

met at the farm said that. 'He told us Maslow had sent him to the farm to look for a dog. He said he came from Ramford City; knew Maslow through the meat business.'

'Oh, you mean *that* Maslow?' I grinned, affably.

Tulley grabbed a handful of shirt and pulled me close.

'I told you once, Lomax, I won't tell you again: don't get smart.' He shoved me back against the door. 'What's Maslow hired you for?'

'He hasn't, and anyway, who hires me is *my* business,' I growled.

Tulley stepped back, looked across at the four siblings and jerked his head towards me. They rose, hitched up their trousers and swaggered over. The one I'd met at the farm, the one called Jack, licked his lips, then, without warning, lunged at me. I half turned. His fist slammed into my chest, rocked me back against the door. I felt the glass panel shatter, then heard the fragments tinkle on to the landing. His brother jabbed me below the ribs. He didn't quite drive all the breath out of me. Maybe he was just being playful. I doubled up, fighting for air. The one called Jack closed in again and drew back his foot to swing a kick at me. I came up fast and slammed him under the jaw. All my weight went into the punch. I felt his body momentarily hang on my fist, then he crashed down on to the low table. Its spindly legs gave way and left him sprawling on the linoleum, amongst a clutter of old magazines.

The rest of the pack leapt on me. I ducked and weaved, threw some punches, tried to fend off the hail of kicks and blows. They were pounding me with a mindless brutality, and I began to succumb.

'Watch it, watch it.' The father muscled his way in and dragged them off me like an old bulldog tossing pups aside.

I sagged back against the wall. There was a warm sticky trickle down the side of my neck that grew cooler as it reached my throat. I wiped at it with the back of my hand, got blood all over my cuff.

The four sons were breathing hard and their eyes were bright. They'd enjoyed working me over. They were excited, keyed up, straining at the old man's leash.

Tulley moved between me and them. 'Maslow,' he snapped. 'You're working for Maslow.'

I shook my head. I wished I'd not. The movement sent a stab of pain zigzagging through my brain. 'I've been to see Maslow,' I said. 'He showed me his dog, but he didn't hire me.'

'You're lying.'

'Do I look as if I'm lying?'

'Yeah,' the sons jeered in unison.

'You'd better not be,' Old Tulley muttered.

I dabbed at the rivulet of blood, glowered at him, held my breath and tried to control the pain.

Presently he said, 'If you're not working for Maslow, who the hell are you working for?'

'That's my business.'

He smashed me across the face, then dragged me upright again and used my shirt-front to wipe the blood from his hand.

'Don't smart-mouth me, Lomax. You're either working for Maslow or the widow. Which?'

'The widow hired me after her husband was murdered.'

'Do a little embalming on the side, do you, Lomax?'

'Huh?'

The old man stayed po-faced, but the sons were sniggering.

'Embalming: she needed an undertaker, not a snooper. Why should she want to hire you?' he said.

'She wanted me to trace some cash her husband had borrowed. The creditors are itching to get it back.'

'Creditors?'

'Maslow and a scrap merchant called Tulley.'

'I'm Tulley, and these are my boys,' he growled.

'Is that so?' I figured there was no point revealing I knew who he was.

'Yeah,' the sons chorused.

'You've been to see Maslow, why didn't you pay me a call?'

'I'd have got round to it.'

He scowled disbelief at me. 'Liar. You did a deal with Maslow. Why else would the old goat keep on at me about waiting a few days before I sent my boys in to see what they could find? Maslow wanted to make sure you got in first, recovered what you could and to hell with me.' He jabbed away at a bruised rib and raised his voice as he demanded, 'I'm right, aren't I, Lomax?'

I winced. The room was swaying like a sunflower in a cyclone. I tried hard to focus on his good eye. 'Wrong,' I muttered. 'You've got it all wrong. The widow hired me to trace the missing cash because she was scared of the creditors. I was just checking Maslow out. I'd have checked you out.'

'What about the farm? Why were you poking your nose into Hawkins's and Jack's little dog-breeding business?' asked one of the sons.

'Saunders used to go there. I'm looking for leads. Anything that will help me find the cash.'

'You'll only find dog-leads down there, Lomax. You're either kidding or you're even more stupid than you look.'

'I think he's kidding us. Nobody could be that stupid.' Another son said that.

'OK, that's enough.' The old man snapped them into silence, then came in close. 'The widow owes me almost half a million, Lomax. Do you know how long it took me to make that kind of money? Do you know how hard me and the boys had to graft to get it together? I don't know why I let Maslow talk me into that stupid time-share flats deal with Saunders.' He glowered at me for a few seconds, then his voice dropped and he spoke slowly, his tone menacing, as he added, 'I'll let you fool around for another twenty-four hours, no more. After that me and the boys will have to move in and recover what we can. And anything you trip over is mine, Lomax. Your arms and legs won't be the only things we'll break if you try and scarper with the cash.'

He turned towards his sons. 'Get Jack back on his feet and we'll clear out.'

The room swayed some more while they trampled around over the remains of the coffee table and the scattered magazines, manhandling the limp-bodied Jack.

Old Tulley looked back at me and growled, 'Where's the widow?'

'Out of town,' I mumbled. 'She's staying with friends.'

'Out of town?'

'She didn't tell me. When she wants me, she just phones or comes into the office.'

He showed me some big teeth. 'You live in a fantasy world, Lomax. You couldn't tell the truth if you tried.' He made a grab for some shirt and went through the pull-me-close routine all over again. Beer-moist breath fanned my cheek as he snarled, 'When she phones you next time, Lomax, just remind her I lent her husband half a million quid. Tell her she'd better get it to me quick.'

His mouth worked itself into something between a grimace and a leer, like he was going to make a dirty phone call, then he added, 'Tell her my boys are as randy as stoats, and greedy with it. A woman as luscious as that, Lomax, ripe, begging for it . . . ' He licked his lips. His voice was low and throaty now. 'Young blokes in their prime. If they've got to come debt-collecting, things are bound to get out of hand.' His leer widened. 'Tell her they'll all give her a real good seeing-to.'

The young blokes in their prime started sniggering. Maybe they were hoping Dad never got his cash back. They trudged past us, crunching over shards of glass, two of them holding up their limp and groaning brother Jack. As they shoved and stumbled through the doorway, the last fragments of glass fell and shattered on the floor. The sons tramped around the landing, then began to crash their way down the stairs.

Tulley heaved me back against the wall. 'You've got twenty-four hours, Lomax, then it's the cash or we're coming for you and the widow. And don't waste any time searching Saunders's place. The boys did that before we came here.'

He crunched out, scowling back at me over his shoulder, and followed his sons down the stairs.

I heard the phone ringing in the inner office. It must have been ringing a long time to cut through the haze of pain and nausea the Tulleys had inflicted. I pushed myself off the wall, limped over to the door, fumbled for the keys and eventually got it open. The phone went on ringing. I began the faltering trek across the carpet, expecting the shrill sound to stop with every painful step. It didn't. I grabbed the receiver, flopped down in the chair behind the desk and grunted

175

into the mouthpiece.

'Mr Lomax? Mr Lomax, is that you?'

'Yeah, it's me, Mrs Saunders.'

'I'm at Vivian's flat. He's just been up to the house to get something for me. He says it's been wrecked: furniture slashed open, beds torn apart, clothes and everything scattered all over. Why, Mr Lomax? Who would want to do such a thing?'

'The Tulleys did it,' I said. 'And they've just paid me a call. They're getting edgy about the money your husband borrowed.'

'But they can't break my home up! I told you I'd pay the money back when you find it.'

'They'll do worse things than smash your home if you don't come up with the cash.'

'If *you* don't come up with the cash, Mr Lomax,' she corrected. 'Don't forget what I hired you for.'

'Yeah,' I said. 'I'm not likely to.' I glanced down. Splotches of blood were dripping on to the papers on the desk.

'Have you made any progress?'

'Progress?'

'Please don't be evasive, Mr Lomax. You know what I mean. Progress tracing the money.'

'None, absolutely none.'

'Have you been to see his first wife? You said you were going to check her out.'

'No. Something cropped up and I didn't make it.'

'Didn't make it?' There was a peevish indignation in her voice now. 'I don't think you're representing my interests very well, Mr Lomax. My home is vandalized and defiled, you don't even have the time to check out a few people, you — '

'Your home won't be the only thing that's defiled if you don't get out of town,' I interrupted. 'The Tulleys have given me twenty-four hours to locate the cash your husband conned out of them, and then they're coming for you and me.'

'*Me?*' she repeated, in a how-dare-they kind of voice. She seemed to have recovered her confidence a little since the weepy session earlier that afternoon, remembered what a pillar of the community she was, how she ought to be looked up to and respected.

'Yeah, and his boys make Attila the Hun and Genghis Khan seem like a couple of drag queens.'

'You mean they'd . . . '

'You know what I mean, Mrs Saunders. So, if you've no more ideas about where your late lamented hid the cash, I'd like to get you out of town fast. In fact, I think you'd be wise to take a flight to Ireland tonight.'

'No,' she snapped defiantly. 'The police are

177

releasing Rex's body in a couple of days. I've got to sort things out and make the funeral arrangements.'

'They'll be arranging *your* funeral if you don't clear out.'

'But surely I'm safe here, in my friend's flat. Only you and Vivian know where I am.'

'They're not stupid, Mrs Saunders. Maslow, Tulley, farmer Hawkins; they all knew your husband, and there must be people in town who know you've got a friend with a flat over the Stirling Street shopping centre. An hour by the telephone, a little legwork, and they'd be rat-tatting on your front door.'

Her rapid, panicky breathing came down the line while she thought that one over. When she spoke again, her voice was softer, less strident, and there was a hint of humbled pride as she said, 'There are other reasons why I can't leave here, Mr Lomax.'

'Such as?' I growled.

'I . . . I can't talk about it over the phone. Can you come over to the flat?'

'OK, I'll come over.' I let that float out on a resigned sigh.

'When? Now?'

I prised myself out of the chair and glanced at the wall clock. It was almost six. I had to clean myself up, change my clothes. 'Give me a couple of hours,' I said. 'I'll be there around eight. And don't open the door to anyone but me.'

I replaced the phone, gathered up the papers I'd bled on to and dropped them into the waste basket. Somehow I managed to bend low enough to open the bottom drawer and snatch out the office bottle. I swallowed a couple of mouthfuls, then took the Scotch with me, cradling it like a baby as I limped out of the office, across the landing and into that shrine to sanitary engineers the landlord calls my exclusive toilet facilities.

I switched on the light and risked a peep in the mirror. A ring on a fist, or maybe a fragment of glass from the office door, had nicked a lump of flesh from my ear-lobe. Blood was still flowing down my neck and dripping off my chin. The shoulder and lapels of my jacket, my tie and shirt-front, were soaked with blood. I did the best job I could of cleaning my face up, then held a wad of toilet paper against the gash to stem the flow. There was an old raincoat hanging behind the door. I slipped it on to hide the bloodstained suit, tucked the bottle of Scotch into the pocket and headed on out. I was pining for home, a hot bath and a change of clothes.

14

I did a few detours and some twisting and turning during the journey back into town. When I eventually parked in the service area behind the pizza parlour, I was pretty certain I'd not been followed. I climbed out and locked up, then stood in the deep shadows beside the car and watched and listened.

Lights were coming on in the flats above the shops. Behind me, an extractor fan was pouring out warm spicy smells, reminding me my last meal was seven hours, a beating, a bath and a change of clothes ago. Its humming almost drowned out the faint sound of distant traffic and the echo of footsteps along the shopping mall. Some youths were shouting, kicking a can along, and I could hear the shrieks and giggles of a bevy of girls out on a spree: the nocturnal sounds and smells of down-town Barfield.

There was nothing strange, nothing out of place, no Tulleys lurking in the shadows, so I headed up the concrete stairs to the access deck and began to make my way past doors and curtained windows to the flat Mona was pretending to hide in.

I'd changed into a crisp white shirt, fresh from the maker's box, and a new silk tie. The only suit I had left was dark-blue, hand-tailored and lightweight. The tip of the blue silk handkerchief that came with the tie was playing peek-a-boo out of my breast-pocket, and the nearly new black shoes were painful. I'd managed to stem the flow of blood from the gashed ear-lobe, but my chest ached with the pounding they'd given me, and walking was painful.

The place was still unfamiliar to me. When I knew I was getting close, I began to note door numbers, then stopped outside the flat and fingered the bell.

'Who is it?' An apprehensive woman's voice came faintly through the door.

I got my mouth up close to the shiny yellow paint job and said, 'Lomax.'

The latch clicked, the door opened a fraction, and one of Mona's big dark eyes was giving me the once-over around the edge of the frame. A chain rattled, the door opened wide, and I stepped inside.

She was wearing an emerald-green dress fashioned in a short and skimpy style. The silky material was close-fitting, tight almost, on the arms, across the bodice, and around the waist. The full skirt swirled out over her hips. It was fastened up the front with tiny, iridescent green buttons. I guess her fingers must have got tired when she was dressing because there were plenty undone at the top. Larger iridescent green studs were clipped to her ears, and her feet were tucked into some silly little gold slippers that were trimmed with green feathers. When she led me into the living-room, I caught a fragrance that was exclusive, but not too restrained.

She gestured towards the chintzy sofa and said, 'Would you care for some tea?'

I sank deep into big downy cushions, smiled at her and told her I would. It was a Scotch I really needed.

She stepped over to a tray on the Ercol table, went through the milk-and-sugar routine, then swirled back with a dainty little cupful. She sat next to me on the sofa, demure, but close. That surprised me. I'd expected her to take one of the matching armchairs.

Vivian had been busy with his blow-wave machine. Her long, nearly black hair was cascading around her shoulders with an artful naturalness. It was crying out to be touched.

She took a genteel little sip at her cup, then almost choked when she saw the side of my face. 'My goodness, what happened to you?'

I grinned at her. 'Someone tore my ear-ring out.'

The dark eyes widened and a disbelieving little smile moved over her lips. She was wearing make-up tonight. She didn't need it, but it wasn't doing her any harm.

'Ear-ring? I didn't think you were the type.'

I nodded seriously. 'They have a language. One says you're available, two says you're spoken for.'

'Really?' She moved her head so she could check my other ear. 'You only had one,' she said.

'Yeah,' I said. 'I only had one.'

I gave her a long steady look. She returned it, the disbelieving little smile still shaping her lips. Her narrow shoulders were thrown back in a kind of defiant challenge to the tiredness and fear that roamed behind her eyes and stalked the beautiful contours of her face. Maybe the powder and paint job was part of her struggle to hide the way she really felt. Close up it didn't stop her looking fragile and vulnerable and near to tears.

'Tell me how it really happened,' she said.

I swallowed a mouthful of the tea. It was an aromatic little something or other that tasted like an infusion of rabbit droppings in rubbing-oil. If it was meant to damp the fires of carnal lust, she'd been conned. No matter how hard I tried, I couldn't stop my eyes from wandering to the smooth tanned flesh

183

straining against the casually buttoned bodice of her dress.

'Shaving,' I said. 'I did it while I was shaving.'

She leant forward, placed her fingers on my cheek and turned my head so she could take a closer look. 'You must do your shaving with a chainsaw.' She took her fingers away. The burning sensation lingered on my skin.

I shook my head and muttered, 'Safety razor.'

'Then you're either still kidding me or you're Yorkshire's most reckless shaver.'

'Don't stint me,' I said. 'My reckless shaving's renowned over three counties.'

She laughed. It was a fragile little laugh that tinkled out and fluttered around the room for a couple of wing-beats, then fell exhausted on to the chintz. Her tiny chin was trembling. She was biting her bottom lip hard. The silly small-talk was over. She said, 'What am I going to do, Mr Lomax?'

'Get out of here. Go back to your folks in Ireland.'

'I won't do that, no matter how bad things get. My pride wouldn't let me. There were some unforgivable things said when I married Rex.'

'Pride is the first thing you'll lose if Tulley and his boys get you. They'll dream up ways of humiliating you that'll give degradation a whole new meaning.'

'The police . . . surely they'll stop them?'

'We've been through all this before, Mrs Saunders. The police couldn't protect you for long against a threat like that, even if they wanted to, and somehow I don't think they'd be too eager.'

'I don't know what you mean.'

'I had strings pulled. Sloane and Mace, the Crime Squad cops, they were told to lay off you. They didn't like it.'

'How did you manage that?'

'Maslow arranged it.'

'I didn't know things like that happened.'

'Nothing's sacred, Mrs Saunders.'

She gazed at me, wide-eyed and scared. Maybe she was beginning to understand how bad her situation was.

'Is there any chance you'll find the money?' she asked.

I frowned down at my cup. The time for protecting a new widow from needless grief was over. 'I've still got to check out your husband's first wife, but I don't expect that to get us anywhere. You're sure there are no banks, no deposit boxes, where he could have stashed it away?'

She gave me a bleak look and shook her head.

185

'The cash won't be in the house. The Tulleys have searched the place in a way I never could, and they found nothing. If they had, they wouldn't still be making threats.' I remembered the unsold flat. Its small size and sparse furnishings meant it would be low on hiding-places, but I made a mental note to check it out again.

'You're sure he's not moved the cash out of the country?' I asked.

'He wouldn't have transferred it through a bank, and he's never been abroad. He hardly ever went out of the area. And he'd no business associates close enough to trust with that amount of money.'

'Did he need it to cover expenses? Pay off debts? He bought a lot of property.'

'He bought a lot and sold a lot, Mr Lomax. You've looked through his personal cash book. On just a few pages I added up more than four million in sales.'

She took a sip at her cup. She seemed to be savouring the aromatic concoction. Maybe it kept her complexion young and fresh looking.

'I wish I'd helped him more, at least shown a little more interest in the business,' she said, half to herself. 'I just enjoyed spending the money he made. Enjoyed the freedom of never having to worry about it. Back home, things were never like that. I had a very ordinary childhood, Mr Lomax. My father was a bricklayer. We lived in a small country town in County Wicklow.'

'You were a model,' I prompted. 'A fashion model.'

Her eyes brightened. 'How did you know that?'

'Doesn't everyone? You were famous.'

She laughed, obviously flattered. 'I don't think so, Mr Lomax. I just had the kind of look everyone wanted at the time. And I was much slimmer then, of course.'

I smiled across at her, tried hard to act the gentleman and keep my eyes on her face when all the time they wanted to drop to the unfastened buttons on the bodice of her dress. I much preferred the mature, more voluptuous Mona.

'You married very young.'

She flashed me a grateful smile. 'Not really. I was twenty-five. I met Rex on a fashion shoot. He was just getting established then. Heavens, he was handsome! He had a specialist firm that did very high-quality shop-fitting work. An art director for one of the fashion magazines got him in to construct some elaborate sets.'

She searched my eyes, suddenly more relaxed. Recalling happier times seemed to have given her a brief respite from care. I didn't try and make conversation. I was aching badly from the beating Tulley's sons had given me, and my gashed ear was throbbing like a tribal drum. But the room was warm, the sofa comfortable and the view sensational.

After a while she said, 'Of course, I was beginning to lose my coltish, adolescent look by then. There's only so much you can do by dieting. And anyway, my parents never did care for me being in modelling.'

I raised an eyebrow.

'They thought some of the clothes I wore, some of the poses, were immodest. They're both deeply religious. I have uncles, aunts, nephews, nieces, who are priests and nuns. And I made quite a lot of money. That made me independent, and I don't think they liked that. They certainly didn't like me going home in skimpy Valentino dresses, driving a red sports car: it raised too many eyebrows. Once when I was there, the parish priest preached a sermon on modesty; said young women should take care not to arouse carnal lusts.'

'He had a point,' I said. 'The local boys must have been at fever pitch. And you could have been giving his curate steamy dreams.'

She laughed happily at that, then suddenly went serious. 'They wouldn't come to the wedding: my parents and relatives, I mean. They sent over an uncle who's a priest to try and talk me out of it. One of my brothers was going to give me away, but they put pressure on him and he cried off at the last minute. Sad, really, but the marriage was good. At least, it was until last year.'

She took some more sips at her tea, gazing at me over the rim of the cup. 'You're married, aren't you, Mr Lomax?'

'I was once.'

'Ah, you're divorced.'

I shook my head. 'Widower.'

She looked contrite. 'I'm sorry. I could tell you'd been married, but I shouldn't have presumed you were divorced.'

'There's a lot of it about,' I said, wondering how her instincts could be so infallible.

I tried to recollect the sights and sounds and events of the past few days. Something was fretting away at the back of my mind. There was a connecting thread amongst the clutter of memories and impressions, but the warmth of the place, pain from the beating and the nearness of Mona Saunders weren't helping concentration any.

I gave up the struggle and said, 'I think it's important for you to get out of Barfield. If you can't go back to Ireland, lose yourself in London. Stay in a hotel until the dust settles.

189

Let your husband's funeral wait.'

'That's the problem I wanted to talk to you about when I phoned. I can't.'

'Can't?'

She looked down at her hands, then said lamely, 'The police told me not to leave Barfield. I suppose I could tell them where I was going and why. I'm sure they'd understand.'

'That wouldn't be a good idea. If your bridge partner, Maslow, can have the Crime Squad pulled off, he's got friends in high places. It wouldn't take him long to find out where you were if the police knew.'

She let out a bleak little sigh and went on staring at her hands.

'Now, tell me the real reason why you won't leave.'

Her face started to crumple, but she took a deep breath and pushed her shoulders back. Somehow the buttons on her dress coped with the strain while she held back the tears.

'It's the usual reason: money,' she said. She was choking back sobs, trying hard to get her emotions under control. 'I've very little left. I've been draining the current account, and I've no idea where Rex drew the funds from to feed it. I should have taken more interest, but I didn't know this was going to happen. I expected things to go on the way they were for ever.'

She looked up at me and waited for a comment. When she didn't get one, she went on, 'I still have the money I had when we married, but it's invested and I need time to sort it out. And disposing of the house and the flat Rex held on to can't be done quickly.'

I put the cup of tepid wart-remover on the floor beside the sofa and mulled over what she'd said. She wasn't stupid, grief hadn't made her irrational, but it didn't make any sense.

'You don't really have a money problem, Mrs Saunders. It's just a short-term cashflow thing. I think you should get a long way from here and run up a bill in a hotel until you can release some cash. Forget what the police have told you to do. They're not going to give you protection, and there's someone at headquarters who could be dangerous.'

'But that's not what I want,' she said stubbornly. 'I'm sure those men are only making threats. They wouldn't dare do those things to me. They'll soon come to their senses and realize they're going to have to wait for their money. And I want to organize the funeral. I owe that to Rex, and no one's going to stop me.'

She'd resumed her pillar-of-society, woman-of-substance roles, and was frowning at me from the far end of the sofa. She couldn't accept that the Tulleys wouldn't give a damn who she was, and lack of cash seemed to be getting to her more than her husband's death or the danger she was in.

I was tired of it all. I'd had my house and office ransacked, a humiliating beating, and I'd not seen a down payment. So I gave her a weary little sigh and said, 'OK, Mrs Saunders. If that's the way you want it. Lock yourself in here, keep the curtains drawn and don't answer the door to anyone.'

We looked at one another for a while, then I tried to inject urgency into my voice as I said, 'The money your husband borrowed meant a great deal to Tulley and Maslow. It would have meant a great deal to almost anyone. Apart from which, they're hardcases feeling sore because they think they've been suckered by a con artist. They're not being playful. They mean what they say.'

'You won't change my mind, Paul. May I call you Paul?'

I said she could, but figured she might get a little sniffy if I called her Mona.

She relaxed back into the upholstery. She'd got what she wanted. She'd be used to that with indulgent old Rex.

'You know, you do remind me of my husband when we first met.' She was looking at me from under lowered lashes now, and her voice had softened. 'He was tall and broad, like you, with lots of dark curly hair. He began to put weight on a couple of years ago and started losing his hair. I don't think I minded too much. It doesn't happen overnight, and you've got time to grow accustomed to it. What I did mind was the way he became less refined. I can't put it into words, but he just seemed to stop bothering about the way he dressed and behaved, and this past year he's been completely indifferent to me. We were no more than brother and sister, going about our separate lives.'

And then it was as if she couldn't hold it back any more. Her face crumpled and she moaned, 'Now he's dead and I'm in this awful mess and . . . oh, God . . . ' She began to let out body-shaking sobs. Through it all I could hear her moaning, 'Help me, Paul. For God's sake, help me.'

I tugged out the blue silk handkerchief and passed it to her. She began to dab her eyes while she choked back sobs and gazed at me in a bewildered, helpless kind of way.

'I feel rotten. I feel as rotten as hell. It wasn't as if being married to him was worth all this worry and pain, not towards the end, anyway.' She reached out and grabbed my hand, and I could feel her warm, soft thigh pressing against mine.

I said nothing, just looked at her and tried not to wince as her nails dug into my wrist.

'What are you going to do about it? I need someone to help me. Help me, for heaven's sake!' She choked out the words with a tearful, self-pitying kind of petulance.

'I think you need someone a little more sensitive, Mona, someone who's good on feelings. Someone like Vivian Delmar.'

'Sod Vivian,' she snapped, and the uncharacteristic coarseness surprised me. 'He'll listen while you pour your heart out — half the married women at the salon use him for that — but when it comes to real help, he's useless.'

Her eyes were half closed now. She'd stopped trying to sink her nails into my wrist and her hand was moving up my arm. Her lips were parted and her breath came brushing against my cheek in shallow little gasps.

I tried to work it out. An old lecher once told me a woman's never more vulnerable than when she's missing the man she loves. And Mona had been missing Rex for much more than the past few hours.

She looked uncomfortable. I lifted her

shoulders off the sofa, eased a couple of big cushions under her and lowered her into them. Some relaxed little sighs told me she liked that.

We just looked at one another. The talking was over. I knew I ought to get up and put some distance between us, but she was sitting very close to me, her fragrant body squeezed into that skimpy green silk dress, her near-black hair all over her shoulders, big eyes half-closed, soft lips glistening and parted. And I suddenly thought, what the hell? I might not want to act like Attila the Hun, but that didn't make me Saint Francis of Assisi, either. And what kind of louse would pile some more bruises on a woman's fragile ego by even pretending he could resist.

Her lips felt just as full and soft and eager as they looked. Slender arms snaked over my shoulders and her fingers began to tangle in the hair at the nape of my neck. I held her tighter, pressing her into the cushions, and she didn't seem to care what happened to her skirt when she slid her legs over my knees.

After a while she pulled her mouth away and breathed, 'You animal. You great big animal,' and began to nuzzle me and moan out a mixture of demands and expletives that would have made a sergeant-major blush.

I didn't have to try too hard to get into the spirit of the thing. It wasn't all that boring. And, like I said, the last thing I wanted to do was heap a bruised ego on top of Mona's pile of problems.

15

It was a plain red-brick box of a house with a roof of pseudo-Spanish tiles. The white plastic window-frames held double-glazing that had been criss-crossed with strips of lead. Someone had done a neat varnish job on the mahogany front door, and slender timber posts held up a canopy that extended across the double garage. Its Georgian style up-and-over door had been painted white, with the panel mouldings picked out in grey.

There was no hedge or fence to separate the house from the street, and turf carpeted the space out front. The joints between the squares were almost healed over. In the middle was a hole the size of a dinner plate, with a young tree planted in it. The plastic tag printed with a long Latin name was still shiny and legible. An estate agent's for-sale board had been fixed at the back of the footpath, and there was a 'Sold Subject to Contract' sticker pasted over it.

Six paces down the path got me to the front door. I gave the brass lion's-head knocker a whirl. I took it easy. I didn't want the ex-Mrs Saunders's dream home to fall apart at the seams.

There was no answer, so I risked a harder pounding.

There was still no answer.

I took a walk across the front, down the side and around the back. As I went, I peered through windows at the turquoise Dralon three-piece suite, big television, blue-and-gold carpet, washing-machine, fridge, tumble-drier: all the technology needed to keep modern man's mind comatose, his body clean and comfortable.

I took a peek in the dustbin by the back door. There were a few food wrappers, a couple of Scotch bottles and maybe half a dozen empty American-dries. I began to warm to Rex's ex. We had things in common.

'Looking for someone?'

I glanced up. A guy of about thirty with sandy hair and a fresh complexion was staring at me over a neatly clipped privet hedge. I gave him my Mr Wonderful smile, the kind of smile a loan-shark gives a housewife before he starts talking about interest, then lowered the rubber lid and dusted my hands off. I walked towards him, trying to look as though snooping in other people's bins was as normal as breathing.

I took my notebook out and found the name Mona had given me. 'Carey,' I said.

'Miss Joyce Carey.'

His face stayed blank. He was short, wiry and neat-looking. New blue jeans and ankle-length rubber boots were peeping through gaps in the foliage, and he was wearing a blue checked shirt. Cotton gloves protected his hands.

'Maybe she calls herself Saunders?' I persisted.

His tiny grey eyes were clouding with suspicion now. 'There's no one with that name here. Who did you say you were?'

'Parkinsons, the Estate Agents,' I said, reciting the name on the board out front. 'I need to talk to her about the sale.'

'Who is it, love?' A woman's voice drifted over the table-cloth-size patch of grass behind him.

'Someone asking for Helen.'

A short girl, aged about twenty-five, joined him by the hedge. Her plump little cheeks were pale and bore the faint scars of adolescent acne. Her brown hair was drawn back and tied with a blue ribbon. She was wearing new blue jeans and a blue checked shirt, too. Matching his and hers outfits. It was only the clothes that matched. Her plump little body was doing things to the jeans and shirt her husband's scrawny frame never could.

199

She folded her arms and looked up at me. I smiled at her. It was one of my hundred-kilowatt specials. She fluttered her lashes like some Sleeping Beauty who's just been kissed by the Prince.

I glanced back at my notebook. 'I think the office must have given me the wrong name or the wrong number. I'm looking for a woman of between forty and fifty.' I figured Rex's first wife would have been in that age range.

'Oh no, that couldn't be Helen,' the husband. protested. 'She couldn't be anywhere near as old as that. She'd be no more than — '

'What do you mean, couldn't be as old as that.' His wife's nasal voice was indignant. 'She's not sweet sixteen anymore.'

'I never said she was. But she's not forty. I bet she isn't . . . '

'And you'd know, wouldn't you?' She glanced across and began to address her remarks to me. 'Garden used to be a mess, then *she* came and I couldn't keep him out of it. Chatting her up over the fence, trimming the privet while she sunbathed. And that's about all she's done this summer. Cut your tie end off once, didn't you, love?'

He scowled and looked sheepish, then wandered off, jabbing sulkily at the ground with the hoe.

She gave me a cocky little smirk. She'd inflicted another tiny defeat, another petty humiliation.

I smiled down at her, wondering how many more he'd stand. I figured Mona must have got it wrong and the best thing I could do was exit gracefully, so I said, 'This is Marsden Road and her name is Carey?'

'No, you're in Marsham Road, and her name's French. Helen French.' She said that in a who's-been-a-silly-boy-then kind of voice.

I took plenty of time looking her up and down, then gave her another great big smile and said, 'I guess you could handle the competition.'

Her body stiffened a little, and surprise registered in her eyes, but I could tell she liked that. Her lashes started to give her plump little cheeks another beating and her tiny, thin-lipped mouth worked itself into a coy smile.

'Lived here long, has she?' I asked.

'Since the house was built, about eighteen months ago. She's only had it up for sale a couple of days and she's sold it already. Kept the price down and threw in the furniture. Been offered a good job in London, lucky cow. Wish someone would offer *me* a good job in London.'

I glanced down the garden. Her husband was some distance from us now, jabbing away with the hoe, savagely annihilating weeds. I figured if he wasn't careful, he'd slice off a toe next time.

'She's not all that old, then?' I asked.

She snorted derisively. 'Don't take any notice of him down there. He's besotted with her. Made an absolute bloody fool of himself, always trying to chat her up, always watching out for her and staring at her over the hedge. She's certainly pushing thirty. Bottle-blonde, fairly tall, always well dressed in a flashy kind of way. My mother would have said she dressed like a tart. She'll be gone the day after tomorrow, so he'll be able to give his eyes and imagination a rest.'

'And I'd better go and find the right property. Sorry to have troubled you,' I said.

'It was no trouble,' she replied. 'No trouble at all.'

I treated her to another smile, closed my notebook, stashed it away, and headed for the car. When I'd settled myself behind the wheel and slammed the door, I took the notebook out again and entered the name she'd given me. I started the engine, reversed in a driveway, then cruised back down the street.

The morning sun was strong now, casting dark shadows under the tiled porches. The identical red-brick houses were crammed on to the tiny plot of land like packing-cases on to the back of a truck. Every bride's dream home: as new as tomorrow, as durable as a paper cup, as overpriced as a big city haircut.

★   ★   ★

It took me less than half an hour to get back to Barfield, park the car and trudge up the rise to the office. After the working-over the Tulleys had given me the day before, I needed crampons and a team of Sherpas to help me cope with the stairs. I dropped the mail on the desk, limped over to the window, heaved it up and leant out. Two floors down, the lunchtime crowd was milling around on the pedestrianized area. Over in the churchyard, gardeners were scything away at bleached grass that waved, thigh-high, around the tombstones. A smell of roasting meat wafted up from the delicatessen. It was tainted by petrol fumes, the smell of sun-baked pavements and ancient grime.

I heard glass tinkle above the background rumble of traffic, turned and glanced through to the waiting room. Melody was picking her way gingerly across the shattered remains of the glass panel from the outer door. I limped over to her, took the lunchtime tray and headed for the desk.

'Spaghetti bolognese, is that OK? Andrea fetched it for you from the Italian take-away.'

'Tell Andrea she's an angel.'

'You only call me angel when you want something,' she said, in a wounded little voice. 'And what's with the limp? Don't tell me you've been tripping over clues again?'

'Just breaking-in some leg-irons for a friend.' I began to struggle with the cardboard cover on one of the aluminium foil cartons.

'I didn't know you had any.'

'Got a cupboard full.'

'I meant friends, silly, not leg-irons.'

I grinned across the desk at her. Her huge baby-blue eyes were giving me a concerned once-over. Her cream silk blouse had full sleeves and the dark-brown skirt was figure-hugging. Tiny crystal buttons that sparkled in the light fastened the blouse at the back of the neck and at the cuffs.

She watched me fumbling with the carton for a few seconds more. When she could bear it no longer, she stepped up to the desk and sighed, 'Here, let me,' then took the hot foil, deftly flicked out the lid, and tipped steaming spaghetti on to the plate. She gave the other carton the same treatment and poured out some red, meaty sauce.

I got my knees under the desk, snatched up the fork and spoon, and began to attack the food while Melody poured out the coffee.

'You've really no idea how to eat it, have you, Paul?' She was ladling sugar into the cup.

'I manage OK.'

'But you're not supposed to put one end into your mouth and keep on sucking until you've cleared the plate.' She took the fork from me, held the prongs in the bowl of the spoon and deftly twirled on a morsel of spaghetti. I opened my mouth, she popped it inside, then went on repeating the process. The perfume on her wrists had a soft flowery kind of fragrance. It suited her. That close, it rode over the savoury aroma of the food.

She suddenly realized what she was doing. 'Here,' she snorted, handing me back the fork and spoon. 'I must be mad. It's bad enough fetching and carrying for you, without feeding you as well.'

'How about my taking you out to dinner again?' I said.

She hitched up the skin-tight skirt and sat down on the far side of the desk. 'I don't think I'd care to have dinner with a man who dates vampires.'

'I'm sorry?'

'Your ear: somebody's bitten half the lobe

205

off. Mona been giving it a little nibble, has she?'

'Oh, that.' I sucked up a length of spaghetti.

'And you know what happens to men who get bitten by vampires, don't you?' she asked.

'Tell me.'

'They turn into werewolves. Mind you, in your case it could only be an improvement. Even a werewolf wouldn't make such a revolting show of eating spaghetti.'

'I guess I'm pretty hungry.' I gave her an apologetic grin.

'How did it happen?'

'I missed breakfast and I was out for elevenses.'

'Your ear-lobe, silly, not your appetite.'

'Shaving cut.' I muttered that through a mouthful of meat sauce. It was hot and succulent.

'You must shave like you eat.' She linked her fingers around her knee and continued to watch me with a kind of revolted fascination.

I put down the spoon and fork, dabbed my mouth with a bile-green paper serviette that bore the legend 'Trattoria Italiana, Barfield', then reached for the coffee. I studied the anatomy lesson perched on the far side of the desk while I sipped at it, and began to smile. Not with amusement, but with pure unalloyed pleasure. Our eyes met. She must have recognized that certain something in my expression, because a faint blush touched her cheeks and glowed through the tan.

She slid off the desk, began to gather up plates and cartons on to the tray.

'I'm off,' she said. 'You look as if you're going to sprout hair and fangs.'

'You should see me when there's a full moon.'

She snatched the cup from me and dropped it on to the tray. 'Take your leg-irons off then, do you?'

I gave her a long slow wink. She picked up the tray and made a dash for the door, teetering on high-heels.

Half-way across the dusty, moth-eaten apology for a carpet she stopped and glanced back at me and said, 'I almost forgot. The police phoned: Chief Inspector Sloane. He asked me to give you a message.'

'Message?'

'He said, 'Tell him Maslow's dead and the hounds are off the leash again.' He said you'd know what it meant.'

207

16

I dragged over the phone and keyed Mona's number while I let the news sink in. Maslow's demise meant one less creditor to hassle her and, if I'd got Sloane's message right, the police were back on the scene. The way things had developed, I figured that could only be a good thing.

The line clicked and a whispery little voice I barely recognized said, 'Hello? Hello? Who is this?'

'Lomax. Is that you, Mona?'

'Thank God. I've been praying you'd call.' I could hear a high-pitched note of hysteria skittering around in her voice, like gritty chalk scraping on a blackboard. She spoke jerkily at first, as if she was choking back sobs or a scream, then the words tumbled out, faster and faster, as she said, 'Men. Some men have been. They were like wild animals. They kicked and pounded on the doors and windows; they've smashed the window in the kitchen. And the things they yelled through the letter-box. Threats, dreadful threats. I still can't believe some of the filthy things they said; things they'd do to me if I didn't pay

208

back the money Rex borrowed.'

'They didn't get in?'

'No, thank God. I wouldn't be talking to you now if they had. I locked myself in the bathroom, but they were yelling so loud I could still hear all the filthy talk. Come and take me away from here, Paul. Please come and take me.'

'Have you phoned the police?'

'No. I only just managed to pluck up enough courage to leave the bathroom and answer the phone because I thought it might be you.'

'OK,' I said, 'I'll come and get you. Pack a few things into a case while you're waiting.'

'But you'll come now?' The panicky voice was pleading with me.

'I just have to make a phone call, then I'll come.'

'No. No phone calls, just get in your car and come straight over.'

'You'll be OK,' I said soothingly. 'They won't come back. If they'd meant to harm you, they wouldn't have wasted time bawling obscenities through your letter-box. They just wanted to scare you to death so you'd hand over the cash if you had it.'

'They certainly did that. Make that call when you get here; just come!' she pleaded.

'I'll be there,' I said. 'Fifteen minutes. OK?'

A faint little 'OK' came echoing back down the line, sounding like a child whimpering in the dark.

I pressed the studs in the cradle of the phone and immediately called Barfield CID. I asked for Chief Inspector Sloane and got put straight through.

'You got my message?'

'Yeah,' I said. 'I got your message. How did he die?'

'That's our business.'

'Some guys visited Mona Saunders this afternoon. Hammering on the doors and windows; yelling obscenities through the letter-box. They terrorized her. She's in fear for her life. Would you say *that* was your business, Sloane?'

'Don't tell me my job, Lomax. It was only a couple of days ago you got Maslow to have us called off.'

'What about taking her in?'

'Why? We don't think she killed her husband. We've no reason to pull her in.'

'For her own protection,' I insisted.

'If she phones and makes a complaint, we'll investigate it.'

'Everyone in Barfield must sleep snug in their beds knowing you're on the job, Sloane.'

'*Mister* Sloane to you, Lomax,' he grated.

And then a note of amusement crept into his gruff Yorkshire voice as he said, 'Have you been home yet?'

'Not since I left this morning.'

'Then I've got more news for you. Some blokes ransacked the place and smashed it up. The neighbours called us when they heard the racket. Uniformed men said they'd never seen such a mess. They wondered if it was frustrated burglars.'

'Frustrated burglars?'

'Yeah. Break in, find nothing worth pinching, so they trashed the place. It does happen. The police who answered the call borrowed a hammer and nails from the neighbour and secured the back door for you.'

'Thanks,' I muttered grudgingly. 'Thanks a lot.'

'And there's one other thing.' He was positively gloating now.

'Yeah?'

'A fax came through last night. Royal Ulster Constabulary pulled someone in for questioning about a bank job in the Republic. They didn't get any sense out of him about the hold-up, but he did tell them something interesting.'

He let it hang there, tantalizing me, waiting for me to ask him more. I did my deep breathing exercises into the mouth-piece and waited back.

'You still there, Lomax?'

'Yeah, I'm still here.' I put a little boredom into my voice.

'He cleared the man they were going to finger for the bank job; said he was on the afternoon flight for Ramford at the time the bank was done. Seems a contract's been taken out on a Barfield bloke and he was flying over to put the seal on it. The grass said it was a private eye who'd got himself mixed up in a million-quid con trick.'

I coughed down the line.

'There aren't all that many private eyes in Barfield, Lomax.'

'And it shouldn't be hard for you to trace this guy from Belfast.'

'You've got to be kidding. We don't know what he looks like, don't know his real name: just a couple of aliases. The Royal Ulster only know him by reputation. The bloke they pulled in called him The Mutilator.'

'Mutilator?'

'Yeah,' came the gloating voice. 'Depends which side of the divide you come from. That's the name he goes by in the North, on account of his being a bit kinky.'

'What do you mean, kinky?'

'Women. He does things; he'll even do

things to the corpse.' He let that sink in, then added, 'In the South they call him Cripple-head. Maybe that's their name for a sadistic psychopath. Northern Ulster had thought they were dealing with two different guys, but they've had intelligence that makes them think they're different names for the one killer. He's good, and he doesn't come cheap. Versatile, too: rigs cars, torches houses, piano-wire strangler, handy with a shooter. We figure you'll be a quick cut-price job, Lomax, on account of the fact that you're just a small-town nobody. You must have upset somebody pretty bad. You must have upset them almost as much as you've upset me.'

I sat there, listening to the noises on the line while Sloane's sinister message sent dirty little rodents of fear scurrying around my brain. I knew I had to ask him, one more time, to give Mona protection. I didn't want to. It was demeaning. Asking favours of a guy like Sloane made me feel like some grimy down-and-out begging for the price of a drink.

I took a deep breath and said, 'Creditors are demanding money with menaces from Mona Saunders. Her husband's been murdered. One of the creditors has just died; maybe he was murdered, too. You say some guys have taken out a contract on me. How do you know the hitman who's flown in from Belfast isn't doing two for the price of one? Maybe he's been hired to take out Mona Saunders as well as me. Don't you think you've a duty to take her into protective custody?'

'Information we get from the place where these blokes do their drinking is that they want to deal with the lovely Mona themselves if they don't get their cash back. It's you the hitman's after, Lomax, not Mona Saunders.'

'They've been round to the place she's staying,' I snarled. 'Terrorizing her.'

'Don't rant down the line at me, Lomax. The folks who live in the flats over the shops in the precinct are always whining about rowdies climbing up on to the access decks and making a nuisance of themselves.'

'You know where Mona's staying, then?'

'Don't upset me more than you already have. 'Course we know where she's staying.'

'Take her into the station. You could find somewhere to bunk her down for a couple of days in that great rabbit warren of a place. She's decorative; she wouldn't be any trouble. Just call it eye-candy for the boys.'

'I'd fill the station with crazy floozies if I took in every woman who ran up bad debts and heard voices through the letter-box, Lomax.'

'I'm only asking you to take one woman in.'

'Is it her you want me to protect, or is it your investment of time in a client? Forget it, Lomax.'

'You're staking her out, using her as bait, aren't you, Sloane?'

'I said, forget it. If she was stupid enough to hire you, she'll just have to rely on you for protection. And if you put another foot out of line, I'll nail you before the Cripplehead guy does.'

★ ★ ★

Mona's huge brown eyes were glazed, almost opaque. Her generous mouth drooped in a lopsided kind of way, and slack shadowy flesh became taut and wax-like as it swept over her cheeks. Terror had altered the contours of her features. Looking at her then was like looking at a stranger.

We were standing in the tiny hallway of her friend's flat. Mona was gazing at me with a kind of forlorn and terrified dignity. I opened out her raincoat and offered it to her. She held the cuffs of her black woollen jumper with her fingers and slid her arms into the sleeves. When she did that, I caught the moist, animal smell of her sweat riding hard over the fading odour of stale perfume. Fear seemed to make her hot and feverish; burn her up like a lost soul.

I grabbed her suitcase, opened the door, glanced right then left along the access deck. The long ribbon of brick and concrete was deserted. She followed me out. I slammed the door, then led her past the shattered kitchen window and past another dozen doors and windows before we turned down the steps that led to the service area.

'Is that your car?' I nodded towards a white, two-seater Mercedes.

She said it was.

'Do you mind if we take yours, instead of mine?'

Maslow's death probably meant the Cripplehead guy was already in town. If he was, he'd have been given a description of my grey Jaguar.

'Not at all.' Her thin whispery voice was dead and expressionless.

While she rummaged in a red handbag for the keys, I let my eyes wander around the service area and along the access deck that projected over it. Everywhere was deserted.

I took the keys, got her door open, threw the case into the back and helped her in. Then I went round the car and slid behind the wheel. The engine was cold. I coaxed it into life, then let out the clutch and we rolled out into a side street. The dashboard clock said 3.30. For the next half-hour I cruised aimlessly around the suburbs, working the unexpected twists-and-turns routine, checking the rear-view mirror for a tail while I told Mona about Maslow and how the cops had refused to take her in. I also told her about the guy Sloane had called Cripplehead.

'Cripplehead?'

'It's a name the security people have for him.' I hadn't mentioned the other name they called him by. She was in too bad a state already. She'd have gone all hysterical on me if I told her the sordid little tricks he got up to.

'But why Cripplehead? I don't understand.'

'Maybe it's because he's a little eccentric,' I offered evasively.

'You mean he's crazy, don't you? Someone who's mad and out of control.'

'It could be just Sloane's way of hassling me,' I muttered.

I mulled things over while we motored through a big housing estate, all the time checking the mirrors for a tail.

Maslow had sounded fit enough when we last spoke. If he hadn't been eaten by his dog, it had to be murder. There was no love lost between Maslow and the Tulleys. Maybe they suspected him of teaming up with Saunders to con the half-million out of them. They certainly felt he'd been holding them off while he tried to grab what cash there was.

The Tulleys knew I'd been hired to locate the cash. By now they'd know I was the guy who'd given their box-man brother a headache. They maybe thought *I* had the cash and was holding out on them, too.

When a family like the Tulleys gets taken to the cleaners for half a million and a brother gets a beating they demand a lot of retribution. It's more than the money; it's a face-saving thing. They'd lose all credibility in the seedy world they operate in if it got about that they were a soft touch. And if Maslow was Cripplehead's first job, they'd sure as hell want him to fix me.

'Do you think the Tulleys killed the major?'

I risked a sideways glance at Mona. Huge bleak eyes were locked sightlessly on the windscreen.

'They're too shrewd to do a job like that so close to home,' I said. 'That's why they called in the hitman.'

'And what about my husband, Mr Lomax? Who do you think murdered him?'

'That's something I keep turning over and over in my mind, but I get nowhere. Maslow and the Tulleys were getting edgy about the loans before he died, but they needed him alive so they could squeeze him for the cash. If he'd died from a beating, it could have been threats gone wrong, but a shotgun says it was a deliberate killing.'

'Do you think this dreadful Cripplehead will come for me, too?' She said that so softly the words were barely audible above the noise of the car. It was as if she was thinking out loud, not really wanting me to hear because she couldn't bear the answer.

I changed down, braked gently, then made a left and began to motor along a road that ran beside a park where kids were happy on slides and swings and playing ball. We were cruising through the fringes of the town now. Most of the faces here are dark, and the turbans and saris made vivid splashes of colour against the grime-streaked brick and slate of the crumbling Victorian terraces.

I glanced at her again. Almost-black hair fell, lank and untidy, on to her shoulders, and her grey raincoat blurred her shape. She was sagging back into the ivory leather, as lifeless and defeated as a marionette without its strings.

'He might come looking, but we'll make sure he never finds you,' I said.

'I can't run and hide forever,' she whimpered. Then her Irish accent became more noticeable, her voice stronger, as she said tearfully, 'Sometimes I think God's punishing me for marrying a divorced man and not being a practising Catholic any more; upsetting my parents, ruining their lives. My marriage goes wrong and Rex is murdered. I didn't stop you when you kissed me in that depraved way last night, and then I'm terrorized by a gang of louts he owed money to. And Rex isn't even buried yet. Dear God, what's happening to me? It must be because I'm so wicked, wicked, wicked.'

She was weeping now, silently, no sobs. Tears escaped from beneath lowered eyelids and washed over her cheeks.

I checked the rear-view mirror, pulled over to the kerb, then watched the traffic cruise past for a while. Nothing slowed and parked up ahead, and there were no side streets for a tail to rest in. I saw a box of pink Kleenex tissues under the dash, reached forward, tugged some out and pressed them into her hand.

She opened her eyes, gave a long, juddering sigh, said, 'Thanks,' and began to dab her cheeks.

'If you let yourself get obsessed with guilt like that, you'll need a psychiatrist as well as a private detective.'

'You don't seem to be a religious man, Mr

Lomax, so I don't expect you to understand,' she said, in a chilly, patronizing little voice.

'Religious or not, I hope God's not some ogre in the sky who'd have your dearly beloved wasted just to have a little dig at you.'

'Now you're being blasphemous.'

I reached up and touched her cheek. She didn't flinch or slap my hand away, so I gently turned her face towards me. She wouldn't look at me at first. She just stared down at the crumpled ball of pink tissue she was holding. Then her lashes swept upwards and the huge, dark eyes gazed at me steadily. She'd hinted I'd forced myself on her the previous night, when all the time she'd been begging me for a little action, pulling me down on her hard enough to bend a girder. I guess she wasn't so obsessed with guilt she wouldn't share it around a little.

'What are you going to do with me?' she asked.

'Hide you in a hotel while I get this thing sorted out.'

'You've given up trying to send me home to Ireland, then?'

'No use wasting the air fare. Your parents' home is the second place anyone really trying would look.'

'Have you any money?' she asked.

I raised an eyebrow. 'Some,' I said. 'Why?'

'Because I don't have any. At least, not until some shares are sold tomorrow. And I'm not going to let you dump me, penniless and looking like this, in some sleazy little hotel miles from anywhere. I'd rather go and stay with Vivian.'

I didn't say anything. She still didn't understand how much danger she was in and how few choices she had. And she either didn't think or didn't care about the mayhem she'd bring down on Vivian's curly little head if she bunked down at his place.

'Are you hungry?' I asked.

She shook her head. 'The thought of food makes me feel sick.'

I gestured through the windscreen towards a cinema about fifty yards down the street. Colourful hoardings and Hindi script said it had been taken over by the local ethnic majority. 'How about spending a couple of hours in there while I sort something out? I'll pick you up about nine, when it's starting to get dark.'

'That's three hours, not two,' she protested. 'And it's an Indian cinema. Who wants to watch Uma Padan and Ramashami Shankar in *Vanrenjunga*?'

'You do,' I insisted. 'Padan and Shankar are

Bollywood greats. They're all the rage from Bombay to Calcutta.'

I glanced up and down the street. Unless the guy from Belfast had a deep tan and wore a yellow turban, he wasn't on to us. I climbed out of the car, walked round to Mona's side and opened her door. I almost had to lift her out.

'I'm not spending three hours in that place,' she said defiantly.

'Come on, Mona. There are things I've got to do. It's dark and safe and no one would look for you in there in a million years.' I got my wallet, pulled out a couple of fivers and held them out to her.

'Look, I'm hiring you and I want you to stay with me, not shove me into that place while you go gallivanting off on your own. If I'm paying the piper, I want to call the tune.'

'I don't remember you doing any paying yet, Mona. And you've got to make your mind up whether you just want me for a little necking when you're feeling in the mood, or whether you want me for protection. If it's protection, *I'm* calling the shots.'

Her jaw dropped a little at that, then her eyebrows came together like a couple of charging rhinos and she slapped me hard across the face.

'How dare you?'

I grinned down at her.

She coloured up fast, then lowered her lashes to hide her embarrassment. When they came up again, she was giving me a long steady look.

I let my grin widen. I must have put the right mixture of insolence and wickedness into it, because she had to pout to kill a smile that was already in her eyes. After a few seconds she gave in, and her lips curved and parted.

'If you just want me for a little necking, you can have me for free,' I said softly. '*Protection* you pay for, Mona.'

'And if you were a gentleman, you'd have forgotten what happened last night. You'd have understood that I'd been so traumatized I wasn't behaving normally. And if you were only *half* a gentleman, you'd be pleased to give me protection for free in return for what you so crudely call a little necking.' She snatched the notes out of my hand, tossed her head, then walked away from me with quick, angry little steps.

Her raincoat was drab and creased. She was wearing red high-heeled shoes and no stockings. I guess they were the first things she'd found to shove her feet into when I'd picked her up at the flat. She crossed the

224

street and headed on. I stood watching her while she climbed the steps and pushed her way through bronze and glass art deco doors into the cinema foyer. She didn't once look back.

17

I drove homewards. I needed to pick up one or two things — that's if there was anything left worth collecting after the place had been ransacked by the Tulleys. I also needed time to think, to get the jittery feelings of panic under control.

Guys on the nine-to-five gravy train were pouring out of town towards me. Up ahead, all three lanes of the inner ring road were clogged with traffic, bumper to bumper, dusty metal gleaming in the fume-blurred sun. I turned and detoured along quieter streets.

The car radio was tuned to the local station. Some fast-patter merchant was reading the five o'clock news. After a while, he gave Maslow's death a mention: said he'd died of gunshot wounds in the grounds of his home, and the police hadn't ruled out the possibility of foul play. I figured that could only mean he'd been murdered. I switched off the set, began to work a little harder at damping down the panic.

The hitman from Belfast couldn't know that Sloane had given me the gypsy's warning about him stalking me. That didn't reduce his advantage much. He still held all the aces. He could pick me off anywhere, anytime. All the knowledge did was alert me to possibilities, make me more jittery. Mona had said you can't run and hide forever, but I figured he wouldn't want to linger long if he'd killed Maslow, and a few days holed up somewhere might do the trick.

As I was driving home I got to thinking he'd try the obvious places first, so I parked the car at the mouth of the cul-de-sac, went round the back of a neighbour's bungalow, crouched low, and moved from garden to garden until I reached my place. My movements were slow and soundless now. I let my face glide past the faded curtains of the living-room window, peering through my own reflection. Sloane hadn't been winding me up. The Tulleys really had worked the place over. There were no signs of movement. Unless the guy they called Cripplehead was crouching down behind the window-sill, there was no one in there.

I moved on past the back door. What damage the Tulleys' jemmy hadn't inflicted, the police had made up for with their botched hammer-and-nail job. Through the window the kitchen looked much the same as it had when I'd last seen it. But then, a herd of stampeding buffalo couldn't make it look any worse.

I headed down the side of the bungalow, past the obscure glazed bathroom window and round to the front. I took a sneaky glance into what had once been my daughter's room. The bare mattress and empty drawers and wardrobe must have told the Tulleys there was nothing there, because they'd gone easy on it. When I got my eye round the rotting frame of the bay window, I saw they'd spent their energies on my bedroom. The mattress had been dragged off the bed and flung against the wall. Sheets, blankets, clothes and splintered furniture had been scattered around the room.

By now I was feeling like a suburban voyeur trying to take in a matinée performance. Unless someone was lurking in the bathroom or the hall, there were no intruders. I got my key, unlocked the front door and shoved it open with my foot. The hall was empty. I stepped inside.

Familiar smells enveloped me. Cloth, paper, dust, the lingering memories of a hundred hasty meals: odours that had seeped into carpets and curtains to mark this place off as my own. The sound of kids playing, lawnmowers mowing, hedge-clippers clipping, drifted in through the open doorway:

normal domestic sounds that emphasized the silence within and made the prospect of danger unreal and remote.

I moved on down the hall and checked the bathroom. There was no one lurking there. I dragged a chair over to the cylinder cupboard, opened a door near the ceiling and groped behind the water tank. The Tulleys had been thorough. They'd found and snatched the wad of emergency funds I keep there. I stepped off the chair, picked my toothbrush up out of the bath, where they'd thrown it, crouched down and used it to probe the narrow gap between the washbasin and the wall. Saunders's cheque-book dropped out.

I went into the kitchen, crunched over crockery, cornflakes, sugar, tea and other stuff they'd tipped on the floor. I needed hot water for a wash and shave. The cylinder was cold, so I filled a big saucepan, put it on the stove and turned the gas up full.

I took a screwdriver with me into the living-room. Saunders's papers were strewn over up-ended furniture, and floor tiles were exposed where they'd dragged the carpet back in their futile search for secrets. I stood there for a while, my back pressed against the wall, listening to my breathing and the almost inaudible pulsing of a clock hidden somewhere amongst the debris on the floor. A frantic inner voice was urging me to get out of that disordered place, filling me with a mindless craving to run.

I worked on the screws at the back of the up-ended television set and pulled off the cover. Saunders's diary and cash book were still there amongst the dust and wires. I fished them out, then heard the hiss of water boiling over on to the stove, and headed back to the kitchen. I grabbed the pan and turned off the gas. On my way to the bathroom, I stepped into the bedroom to salvage a shirt from the chaos.

The mattress rolled away from the wall with a slow, dream-like movement, and its falling fanned me with a rush of air. I could see him now. He was sitting on a mound of blankets and pillows, his back against the wall, a smile on his face. He held the pistol with both hands, arms straight out, just like a pro. As he raised the gun to my chest, his smile widened.

I hurled the pan and threw myself down, heard the muffled crack as the pistol fired, his shocked intake of breath and then the howl as the scalding water seared his flesh. I reached out, grabbed his ankles and jerked him hard towards me. The pistol cracked again as he lost the support of the wall and slid on to his back. I scrambled over him, icy shock and fear melting into white-hot rage. I grabbed the wrist of his gun hand, drove my knee hard up under his ribs, let my two hundred pounds rest there while I punched his face and throat.

Through the frenzy of hate, faintly, as if from a distance, I could hear the gun firing into the bed, his groaning, my own guttural snarling.

He twisted and managed to roll me off him. I felt him straining to turn the gun on me. I let my hand slide from his wrist to the barrel of the gun, felt the hot metal jerk when he pumped the trigger. I wrenched the gun back. He had to let it go now, or his finger, trapped in the trigger-guard, would break. He dragged his hand free and I rolled forward into a trough between the mattress and the bed, then felt him trampling over my legs as he made a dash for the door.

Staggering up, I lurched after him, saw him escape through the front door and start sprinting along the cul-de-sac. He was slightly built, with a black suit, black shoes and plenty of straight blond hair.

Judging by the way he was able to move after the boiling-water treatment and the beating, he was quite an athlete. I slammed the door, then felt the metal silencer of the gun hot in my hand and threw it on the floor. I guess we'd both had our fingers burnt.

The adrenalin rush ebbed away during the walk back to Mona's white Mercedes, and with it the anger and energy it had released. I felt scared and sick and tired of the whole lousy mess I'd been stupid enough to get embroiled in.

I slid behind the wheel. I was almost out of cash, completely out of bright ideas and the Tulleys had trashed the place I call home. I got to thinking the flat Rex Saunders hadn't sold was just about the only place within a short driving distance where Mona and I could hole-up for the next twenty-four hours. After seeing Hawkins's bruised wife there and listening to her conversation with her lover, I'd worked out that Saunders must have loaned it to his friends for furtive little assignations. I figured the initials and times in his diary were booking-out details. Maybe he did it to repay business favours, or to make guys feel obligated. With Saunders dead, there was no one to allocate time and work out a rota. His happy little band of dedicated fornicators would have problems using the place without Rex to organize things and prevent double-bookings. And his violent death would probably make them too scared to go there now.

I cruised around for a while, checking the rear-view mirror. When I was sure I wasn't being followed, I stopped off at a corner store and off-licence, bought some groceries and a bottle of Scotch, then headed for the flat.

Like the first time, I parked well down the avenue, walked back and let myself in with the fancy latchkey. The place was just as I'd left it a couple of days earlier, the négligé and sandals, the dress shop bags, still strewn around the bedroom.

I gathered them up, found the way out into the back yard and tipped them into a communal dustbin. A couple of cars were parked there now, a Toyota and a Volkswagen Beetle. When I got back inside I stood and listened, heard the muffled sound of a noisy Western on the television set in the flat above. I put the bag of groceries in the kitchen, closed the curtains and blinds, then went out the back, across the yard and down an alleyway to the car.

For a while I just sat inside Mona's Mercedes. Shock and fear were really kicking in now, and I had to grip the wheel to stop my hands shaking. My gaze flickered along the suburban street, peering into the evening shadows between parked cars and in all the gloomy doorways. I even looked over my shoulder and checked the luggage well behind the seats.

A cold wind was scattering the first fall of leaves over the road. The occasional car cruised past, but there was no one out walking. It was as orderly and quiet as a street in one of Barfield's better suburbs should be.

18

I parked just beyond the pool of light spilling out of the Cinema foyer. The sky had darkened now and streetlamps were flickering on.

She came down the steps dead on time, hands thrust deep into the pockets of her crumpled raincoat, a worried frown on her face as she glanced nervously this way and that.

I opened the passenger door and waved at her through the windscreen. She looked around when the starter whirred, then came over to the car and climbed inside. I let out the clutch and accelerated hard down the street.

'How were Uma Padan and Ramashami Shankar?'

'Tender and beautiful, but the culture gap was too wide. Three minutes would have been pleasant: three hours were sheer torture.'

We drove along in silence for a few moments. I was constantly checking the rear-view mirrors.

'Are you taking me to a hotel?' she asked.

'A while ago you said you didn't want

dumping in a hotel.' I made right and left turns at speed, jumped some lights, then merged with the traffic on the inner ring road. 'I'd like to take you to one of your husband's flats, one he never managed to sell.'

'Where is it?'

'Somewhere not far from here.'

'I'd rather you took me to another town and put me in a hotel.' Her voice was edgy with alarm.

'It's OK. The Tulleys aren't likely to come nosing around, not in a million years. And I'll be with you. I'm not leaving you on your own.' I tried to sound reassuring.

'You're staying? You're staying the night?' A faintly outraged tone had mingled with the fear in her voice. 'I wouldn't care for that, Mr Lomax. If you're not taking me to an out-of-town hotel, I'd prefer to stay with Vivian.'

She'd stopped calling me Paul. Maybe she was trying to get the relationship back on a mistress and servant basis. And her short and convenient memory was fooling her into worrying more about my animal instincts than her own needs and inclinations.

'His place is only a few doors along from your friend's flat. Anyone watching will have seen you going in and out. Anyway, why involve Vivian in a mess like this?'

She didn't answer that one, just fiddled nervously with the big gold catch of her bag while I drove on towards her late husband's time-share love-nest.

'Just because I don't want to be left alone, doesn't mean I want to spend the night with you. I know attitudes are more relaxed now, but I do have a position to maintain, and some of the people I mix with are still fussy about one's behaviour.'

She was doing her gorgeous school-ma'am act again, treating me like the kid who's just pulled a really big bogey out of his nose. I hadn't told her about my brush with Cripplehead. I didn't want to make her more scared than she already was, and anyway, she wasn't the only one who needed a bolthole for a few hours. I had to find somewhere to get myself together and do a little thinking.

I glanced at her. She was just a dark shape in the darkness of the car. I was tempted to remind her how eager she'd been the night before, how she'd made all the running, then thought better of it. It must have been a kind of hysteria that had made her abandon her natural reserve. Reminding her about it again would only make her even more difficult to deal with.

'What's so special about Vivian?' I reasoned. 'Won't tongues wag if you spend the night with him?'

'Vivian does the hair of almost every woman I socialize with, Mr Lomax. They understand his nature and wouldn't give it a second thought. But one look at you and they'd all jump to the same conclusion.'

'They won't get to look at me. Don't worry, Mona. You can lock yourself in the bedroom. I'll bunk down on the sofa in the sitting-room.'

'I'd rather you didn't call me Mona, Mr Lomax. I'd feel much better if you called me Mrs Saunders.'

'I'll call you anything you damn well please,' I growled. 'Calling you Mona doesn't mean I'm planning to ravish you. I don't force my attentions on women.'

'Really? I found you extremely forceful last night.'

Something snapped inside me when she said that. I'd taken a beating, had my home wrecked, my cash stolen, narrowly missed Cripplehead's ticket to oblivion, and I still had to extricate us both from the mess her husband had landed us in. And she hadn't paid me a penny yet. Maybe she never would. High-class dames don't usually expect the knight-errant business to cost them much more than a flutter of the lashes and the kind of coy little smiles they learn to make on their mother's knee.

I braked hard, pulled over to the kerb and shoved my door open.

'That's not the way I remember it, Mrs Saunders. It was *you* that decided to take your dress off because you didn't want to get the expensive little Dior number crumpled. And it was *you* who said we'd be more comfortable if we put the cushions on the rug. Shall I go on?'

'Shut up! Shut up!' she snapped. 'You don't know what you're doing to me. Can't you imagine how I feel after letting you do that to me?'

'*Letting me?* We're still not thinking straight, are we, Mona? Do you think I didn't know what was driving you? Do you think I'd have held back if I'd thought you were behaving normally?'

'Held back?'

'Yeah, held back. Or have you forgotten what you kept begging me to do? The way you kept dragging my hands to where you wanted them to be.'

She glared at me for what seemed like an age, then hissed, 'You pig,' and slapped me hard. 'You uncouth pig,' and slapped me twice more. 'You filthy . . . '

I saw her hand coming up for a few more slaps and grabbed her wrist. She was a big girl and she wasn't being playful, and I'd had just about all the aggravation I could take for one day.

She gave a little squeal. 'Don't! You're hurting me, you're . . . '

'It's obvious my being around distresses you, Mona, so I'll blow and you can drive this fancy heap anywhere you please. Why not try some of the folks who are still fussy about one's behaviour? Maybe they'll bunk you down for the night and give you a little protection.'

I let go of her wrist, slid out of the car and slammed the door so hard it almost fell out the other side. I strode off down the pavement, looking for a phone-box that would get me a taxi to my car. I figured I could drive somewhere remote and safe and spend the night in it.

I crossed over a junction and began to head past shops that were shuttered and a terrace of mean-looking houses, then I heard the patter of running feet behind me.

'Mr Lomax, don't leave me,' she panted. 'Paul, please . . . I'm just upset. I'm being stupid.'

I felt her tugging at my sleeve and turned and faced her. She gazed up at me with an imploring look and whispered, 'Please, Paul.'

'You're no longer married, I don't have a partner, you were scared and distressed: I don't see what's wrong with finding a little comfort, taking a little consolation.'

'You're not making me feel any better, Paul. I'd only been a widow a few hours when I let . . . when we behaved like that. It made me feel soiled, that's all. After you'd left, I was ashamed: disgusted with myself. I just can't get it out of my mind.'

'I can't forget it either, but the memory doesn't make me feel embarrassed or ashamed,' I said gruffly.

Her face was all dark shadows and I couldn't make out her expression. She didn't speak for a while, but she'd slid her hand up the lapel of my jacket and was clinging on to me. Presently she said, 'Take me to that flat, Mr Lomax. If you think it's safe, I don't mind going there, so long as you'll stay with me.'

She seemed to have changed her tactics; decided to try another technique from her man-manipulating repertoire. She was using her warm, urgent, appealing voice now, and injecting just the right amount of helplessness into it.

I gazed at the dark planes of her face for a while longer, just to keep her on tenterhooks, then led her back to the car and helped her to get inside.

'I must say, I'm a little surprised, Paul.'

'Surprised?'

'That you don't have a partner.'

We were driving through less brightly lit streets now, closing on Saunders's flat. 'There's a woman I'm more than fond of, but she's happy with her life as it is and I don't think she wants the hassle I'd bring.'

'Hassle?'

'Widower with memories, and the job I do. And I think she'd like someone more cultured and refined.' I didn't like telling her that.

Mona let out a little sigh. 'Men aren't perfect. You either get sweet and boring, or big, bad and dangerous to know.'

I began to chuckle softly. 'Which category would you slot me into?'

'You don't really have to ask me that, do you, Paul?'

I drove straight in this time, down the alleyway and parked in the rear yard. The Volkswagen had gone and a big, top-of-the-range Ford saloon had taken its place.

I left my grip in the car, just carried her suitcase and held her arm while I steered her through the darkness, past the dustbins, to the back entrance.

While I was searching for the long master key that opened the outer doors, she said, 'Is she very attractive?'

'Is who very attractive?'

'The woman you're sweet on.'

I didn't care for her question. It upset me somehow. I found the key and slid it into the lock, then said, 'I wouldn't discuss you or your appearance with anyone, Mona. If you don't mind, I'd rather not talk about her in this way.' I got the door open and we stepped into a rear lobby.

She laughed. 'Really, Paul, we'll make a gentleman of you yet.'

She'd recovered her composure, was starting to patronize me as she tried to take hold of the reins again. 'It's the blonde woman in your offices, isn't it?'

'How did you work that out?'

'Just a woman's intuition.'

'You should be doing my job,' I muttered, leading her through the door of the flat and into the sitting-room. 'How about something to eat? I got some bacon and eggs and other stuff.'

'That would be wonderful,' she said. 'But I must have a bath first.'

I handed her the suitcase. 'The bedroom is the first door along. There's plenty of towels in the cylinder cupboard next to it. The bathroom's at the end.'

She kicked off her shoes and limped down the hallway. I switched on the electric fire and headed for the kitchen.

Her scream tailed off into a moan before it really got going, and I heard the thud of a body hitting the floor as I was dashing down the hall. Mona Saunders was lying in a heap on the carpet just inside the bedroom door.

I looked into the room. A woman was spread-eagled over the rumpled bed, on top of a mound of pillows, big eyes wide and shocked, black hair in fine plaits decorated with blue and gold beads. She was tall, very tall, and her naked body gleamed like oiled ebony in the subdued light. It was Maslow's maid, Gloriana. A naked white guy was sprawled, face down, across her legs, his head and arms hanging down over the side of the bed.

I stepped over Mona and closed in. There was a bullet-hole just above the woman's right breast. She hadn't bled much. There was a hole at the back of the man's head and blood had poured from his mouth to form a congealing pool on the carpet. I crouched down beside him, grabbed the hair over his brow and lifted his head until I could see his face. The bullet had entered at the back and made an exit at the side of his nose, leaving a pulpy mess of torn flesh. A mouth full of bloodstained teeth sagged open; eyelids drooped, half-closed, over the kind of sightless eyes you only ever get to see on dead men. I let his head drop back and stood up.

Dark curly hair, just tinged with grey, big features, broad shoulders, six-one maybe six-two tall, weight about two hundred pounds, and only a dim glow from the bedside lamp. Working out what had happened wasn't difficult.

I laid the back of my hand between his shoulder blades and then against the side of her throat. The flesh seemed cool, almost cold. When I took my hand away her head rolled slackly on to its side down the slope of the pillow. I slid my hand between the small of her back and the sheets. Warmth still lingered there. The smell of cordite was strong in the room: stronger even than her perfume, his aftershave, the salty-sour smell of sweat and blood.

I heard a groan behind me, turned and saw that Mona was beginning to surface from a dead faint. I got my arms under her, lifted her, carried her into the sitting-room and laid her on the sofa, then fetched a glass and the bottle of Scotch from the kitchen.

She sprawled limply on the cushions, dark hair lank and tousled, face pallid and sheened with perspiration. Her slack mouth twitched as she made quick little moans, like a sleeper in the grip of a nightmare.

I unfastened her raincoat, eased her into a sitting position, poured out some Scotch and pressed the rim of the glass to her lips. I tilted it until a few drops ran into her mouth. She coughed and spluttered, then started to revive.

'Did I really see that in the bedroom? Are there really two dead people in there?'

'Yeah,' I said. 'You saw them and they really are dead.'

'Who are they?'

I looked her straight in the eye. I figured she could manage very well without the truth. She wouldn't want to know her husband let his friends and business associates borrow the place for the occasional happy hour of love and romance. I said, 'I guess they're the owners and I got it wrong. He must have sold the place, after all.'

'But who would want to kill them?'

'I think someone mistook the guy for me.'

'You?'

'Yeah, me. I came here about an hour ago to look the place over before I brought you. On the way I did plenty of manoeuvring, but the tail must have clung on. I entered by the

246

front, left by the back. The couple through there probably parked in the rear yard and came in the back way. Anyone watching from the street wouldn't see me go out or them come in. The guy has my height and build, similar hair and features. The bedside lighting is low and they were naked. Maybe the killer only got a back view; he certainly wouldn't bother to check for birthmarks before he pulled the trigger.'

'You mean this Cripplehead really is hunting you?'

She was trembling now. I decided it was best not to tell her about my earlier encounter with the black-suited blond from Belfast. I made her nuzzle the whisky some more and tried to sound nonchalant when I said, 'It seems like it.'

'What are we going to do?' she asked in a small, whispery voice.

'The killer won't know he's wasted the wrong guy. We could stay here.'

'With those dead people through there?' She gave a genteel little shudder.

I gave her a tired look. We were running out of options and I was running out of ideas. 'The Tulleys have already ransacked my place. That probably makes it safe enough for us to stay there tonight. How do you feel about that?'

'What about the police? We've got to report . . .'

I shook my head, refilled the glass, took a mouthful myself. When I offered it back to her, she declined. She seemed to have a new-found revulsion at sharing things physical. 'If we call in the cops, whoever did the killing will know it wasn't me by noon tomorrow. We've got to leave them there, let it buy us a little time.' I drained the glass, splashed in some more, drank it, then said, 'You wait here.'

I headed out and down the narrow inner hall, got a towel from the cylinder cupboard and began to wipe places we might have touched. I went into the bedroom, picked up Mona's suitcase and gave the doorknob the treatment with the towel.

An imitation fox fur coat was draped over a chair, and a flower-patterned dress and white silk underwear were folded neatly on top of it. The guy's jacket, socks, shirt and pants were just strewn all over the floor. The subdued light from the bedside lamp intensified the darkness of her skin. In contrast, the broad sweep of his back and buttocks seemed lily-white and bloodless. A regular honky.

On my way back through the hall, I picked up Mona's red shoes and took them in to her. I helped her up, steadied her while she got her feet into them, then stashed the bottle of Scotch and the glass in the bag of groceries. We went out the back way, into the night, hurrying across the yard to the car.

Gloriana wouldn't be handing round the brandy and cigars any more, and I'd never get to read her that bedtime story.

19

Mona didn't try to hide her distaste when she stepped inside the place I call home. But then, it hadn't seen a woman's tender care for almost seven years, and the Tulleys hadn't bothered to tidy up after searching the place.

'This is where you live?'

'This is it.' I made my voice defiantly cheerful as I led her across the minuscule hall into a sitting-room that looked like the inside of a rubbish skip. 'The Tulleys made a mess of it. It's usually pretty shipshape.' I was lying heroically.

'I hope they haven't done this to my home. I've not been there since Vivian told me they'd paid me a visit.'

I tugged the carpet straight, got the sofa back on its feet and gathered up the cushions. When I'd helped her out of her coat, she sat down on the edge of it. She was wearing her bridge-player's outfit: the thing Melody had called a twin-set and the tweed skirt. Sitting there, hands in her lap, knees pressed tightly together, she looked every inch the prim village school-ma'am.

'Don't take your shoes off. There's broken glass everywhere.'

She was staring at the stained threadbare carpet, the faded wallpaper. I suddenly saw it through her eyes and felt ashamed. I should have bothered more, had the decorators in, hired a cleaning-woman. But I'm not a nine-to-five guy: I just use the place to snatch a meal and sleep, and you don't notice how grubby and tired-looking everything gets.

I turned on the gas fire and central heating, lifted the curtain-rod back into its cradle and sealed out the dark.

'How long did you say your wife had been dead, Paul?'

'I didn't.'

I sorted out an armchair for myself, got the bottle of Scotch and a couple of glasses, and fixed her a drink.

'Talking about your wife upsets you, doesn't it, Paul?'

I gazed at her across the splintered remains of a coffee table. She was the first woman to get inside the place since the funeral, and it wasn't turning out to be a happy experience. 'It's not something I'm comfortable with,' I muttered.

She let her eyes roam around the shabby room again, and I began to understand what

Rex Saunders had meant when he said she sometimes made him feel edgy.

'She died almost seven years ago,' I said softly. 'I tidy the place up, clean it now and then; but apart from the grime, and wear and tear, it's just as she left it.'

'You miss her a lot, don't you?'

I didn't answer. She must have known I didn't want the conversation. Probing me like this was almost an act of malice. I sipped my drink and went on looking at her.

'I feel bad about Rex, but I don't think I'm going to pine for him. Do you think that's because I never really loved him?'

'Like I said before, Mona, this isn't my territory. You need someone who's into emotions and feelings. When things get sorted, you ought to go and have a blow-wave and trim so you can talk it over with Vivian.'

She pressed her lips together and gave me a frosty look. 'You know, Paul, I think you're the coldest, hardest, most cynical man I've ever met. My husband was remote and insensitive, but you . . . '

I grinned across at her, pleased I'd put a stop to the personal questions; stopped all the bleeding-heart stuff she was trying to lay on me.

'Can I have a bath?'

'Another fifteen minutes. The water should

be hot by then. I'll go and sort out the bathroom.'

When I crossed the hallway, I saw the gun I'd tossed down amongst the clutter when Cripplehead had legged it. I picked it up, unscrewed the silencer, then let the weapon rest in my hand. It was hard and cold and heavy. Cyrillic script said it was Russian-made. I checked the magazine, saw there were three rounds left, then slid it into my jacket pocket.

Clearing shattered jars and bottles out of the bath and making sure there were no splinters of glass took a little time. When I went back, I saw she'd made the tiny kitchen look clean and tidy.

'They smashed most of your crockery.'

'There wasn't a lot to smash,' I said wryly. 'The water's hot now, and you'll find clean towels in the cylinder cupboard. I'll make the bed up for you.'

She suddenly looked away when I said that, just squeezed past me and headed for the bathroom.

I finished my drink and poured another while I listened to Mona splashing around in the tub. When I thought I'd given her plenty of time, I rustled up some bacon and scrambled eggs and a pot of tea. I laid out the dining-table. It was a first. I usually eat standing up, straight out of the pan. Christmas Days and Sunday, I have a tray on my knee.

Mona drifted in, rosy cheeks peeping out above the collar of my white bathrobe. 'I hope you don't mind my using your robe. I was so upset when you picked me up, I hardly knew what I was doing and I put next to nothing in the case. I took one of your pyjama jackets, too. I hope that's OK.'

I said it was and told her to help herself to bacon and eggs.

She slid on to a chair, pushed up the sleeves of the robe and began forking rashers on to a plate.

'God, I'm hungry. I've never been so hungry,' she said, and began to devour the meal with a kind of ravenous gentility. In the oversize robe, hair loosely pinned up to keep it dry, pink-cheeked after the bath, she looked ten years younger.

I went into the kitchen and collected the tea-making paraphernalia. When I came back, the bathrobe had parted below her waist, exposing long legs and white satin pants peeping out from beneath my striped pyjama jacket. I dragged my eyes away. This was the wrong time and the wrong woman, and I needed that kind of stimulation like I needed a broken leg.

I poured her a mug of tea, then began to eat some food myself. She'd left me a couple of the smaller rashers and a spoonful of scrambled egg. Deep down, hearty appetites surged in that dark pool of guilt and repression.

It wasn't midnight yet, but I was dog-tired, wanting sleep to claim me so the day would end, so I could forget for a few hours the guy they called Cripplehead and the vision of those endless legs emerging from skimpy satin pants.

'I fixed you a bed. There might be some glass left on the floor, so you'd better keep your shoes on.'

'Can't we talk for a while? No one's talked to me for ages. Tell me what you're going to do about this dreadful mess.'

I gave her a tired smile. I'd no idea what I was going to do. Go through the motions of checking out Saunders's first wife, try and stay alive. I couldn't think of anything else. I said, 'We could both use a little sleep, Mona. We can talk in the morning.'

'Let's just clear things away and do the dishes. You can wash, and I'll dry.'

Being squeezed into the tiny kitchen with the near-naked Mona wasn't a good idea. And I didn't care for the domestic fun and games she was organizing, either. 'Leave them tonight. It'll be OK.' I daren't tell her I usually left dishes in the sink for upwards of a week.

'You're pushing me away, aren't you? Rex did that all the time. He didn't want to talk to me, or touch me. There were times when I thought he didn't even want to look at me. What's wrong with me? You're a man: tell me what's wrong with me.'

'Nothing,' I said. 'Absolutely nothing.' I was really wilting now. I couldn't handle any more of this heart-to-heart stuff. 'And you got your husband all wrong. When he hired me, he kept on about how beautiful you are. I think he must have loved you very much. He was feeling his age, that's all. And maybe he was becoming scared and worried about Tulley and Maslow. He got paranoid and thought you were having an affair. Most guys would get distant, leave their wives alone, if they suspected they were cheating.'

'That might explain the last few months, but he didn't touch me for more than a year. And I really mean not touch. He never held me, never looked at me, never said an affectionate word.'

'This isn't my territory, Mona. As far as I can see, there could be only one reason why he was distant. He thought you were cheating. That's why he hired me.'

256

'*Distant*! That's not the word I'd use. And there *is* another reason. It's the universal reason: he was having an affair himself. He'd had another woman for at least a year.'

I sighed, tired of endlessly raking away at the same old plot of ground. I didn't try to hide my exasperation when I said, 'You're not being rational, Mona. If what you're saying is true, what would he hire me for?'

'God knows. Perhaps he thought that if he was cheating, I could be, too. Men who behave like that are usually the most jealous and suspicious.'

I looked across the table at her, desperate for the conversation to end. No matter how beautiful she was, if she'd hammered old Rex like this at every opportunity, he was bound to have gone a little cool. I managed a gentle smile as I said, 'This is something I'm not good at, Mona. I've really no idea why your husband would ignore you the way he did.'

'Would *you* ignore me, Paul?'

Alarm bells were ringing now. I pretended I hadn't heard that one, made my voice brisk, as I said, 'Let's call it a day. I'll grab a duvet from the spare room and kip down on the sofa. If you're scared, you can leave the doors open.'

'Would you?' she insisted, like a dog worrying a bone.

'This conversation isn't a good idea, Mona. You've been traumatized and you're exhausted, and that's making you obsessive.'

'You want me to leave you and go to bed?' she snapped frostily.

'It would be the best thing for both of us.'

The look she gave me mixed reproach and loathing in equal measures. Without another word, she pushed back her chair and headed out of the room.

I listened to her moving around for a while. When everything went quiet, I checked the doors and windows, collected the duvet, stripped down to my boxers and stretched out with my legs hanging over the end of the sofa. I pushed the gun between the cushions and left a table lamp on so I could see if I had to move around in the night. Cripplehead would be thinking he'd killed me. With any luck he'd be on a plane, heading back to Belfast.

★ ★ ★

Mona calling my name and shaking my shoulder roused me. I jerked up.

'There's an awful banging. It sounds like guns firing. I'm scared, Paul.' She was kneeling by the sofa, huge brown eyes staring out from under a mass of tousled hair.

258

I listened to the sound and checked my watch. It was a little before one. 'It's fireworks,' I said. 'Not guns.'

'Who'd let off fireworks? Bonfire Night's more than a month away.'

'It's over the tracks, on the big housing estate. Dealers are telling their customers they've had a delivery.'

'Dealers?'

'Drug-dealers. It's what they do when they've had a drop.'

'Can't they just phone everyone?'

I laughed. 'Take too long. More importantly, the cops could trace the calls. And some of the customers will be too far gone to use a mobile. It's simple and effective, like jungle drums.'

'How do you know this?'

'I gather all sorts of useless information in my business.'

She rose to her feet and stood in the glow of the table-lamp, looking down at me. My pyjama jacket was like an overcoat on her and it was hanging open. Apart from the lace-trimmed satin pants, it was all she was wearing.

'I'm scared, Paul.'

'You're OK. I'm here. Just leave the doors open.'

'I don't want to go back in there.'

'You're not being sensible, Mona.'

'I'm scared, and I want you to hold me.'

'This is ridiculous,' I grated. 'Tonight you want me to hold you. Tomorrow, you'll be on another guilt-trip.'

'Sod tomorrow. No one's held me for months. I'm scared and I want you to put your arms around me.'

'I'm not Vivian, Mona.'

'And I don't care what happens, so long as you put your arms around me and hold me.'

'Go back to bed.' I tried to make my voice reasonable. 'I'll bring the duvet and sleep across the doorway.'

She suddenly squeezed down on to the sofa beside me, started to whimper as she grabbed my arm and tried to pull it around her.

'I'm scared, Paul. Don't push me away. Don't *you* push me away, too.'

I didn't feel good about myself, but what would you have done? How many times and in how many ways did I have to tell her the whole thing was a really bad idea?

The sofa was doll's-house size and stuffed with broken springs, so I wrapped the duvet around her and led her into the bedroom. When I was holding her in my arms and she'd tangled her legs in mine, I forgot the Tulleys and Cripplehead and the whole lousy mess we were embroiled in.

20

Watery sunlight flickered between foliage drenched with rain; tyres hissed through puddles that stretched across the narrow country road. I wasn't used to being out and about before the milk crates started rattling, but I had to make one last attempt to contact Saunders's first wife.

I'd left Mona curled up in the bullet-holed bed. At least, I presumed she was curled up in the bed. I'd spent a long time getting my arm from under her, untwining my legs from hers, so I didn't wake her.

Red brick and Spanish tiles loomed up, throbbing like an abscess on the backside of the sleeping country town. I turned into the estate, parked opposite the house and wound down the window. The dawn chorus hadn't chirped itself out yet. I got my notebook, thumbed through until I found the name the neighbours had given me, then climbed out of the car and strolled over.

The 'for sale' board had gone, but the joints in the turf were still healing and the tree with its plastic name-tag was still fighting its way through the hole in the lawn. Curtains

261

were drawn across windows, the garage door was up and a new-looking red hatchback was parked inside. I pressed the brass bell-push, which matched the Georgian-style knob and knocker and letter-box.

After a while I pressed again, long and hard. I retreated a few paces down the path and stared up at the bedroom windows. A curtain twitched aside and fell back without my having seen anything through the parting. I waited some more. No one came down. I gave the bell another workout and pounded away on the knocker. The racket was loud enough to wake the street.

A window opened. I looked up, saw a mass of auburn curls around a pale oval face. She was holding a crimson robe tightly around her throat. Rings with pea-sized stones were sparkling on plump, tapered fingers.

'Well?' She hissed the word at me.

I took my wallet out, held it up, gave her a quick glimpse of the visiting-card behind the celluloid, then flipped it shut.

'Miss French?'

She frowned, chewed her lip, then said, 'What do you want?'

'Saunders,' I said. 'I have to talk to you about Rex Saunders.'

'You do realize what time this is?' Her nasal voice was low and angry. She'd put a lot of effort into refining the Yorkshire accent, but she wouldn't have made a news-reader.

I smiled up at her. 'Perhaps I could come in and talk?'

Her frown became a scowl. She chewed her lip some more and glared down at me while she thought about it. I kept up the smile. Presently she said, 'Wait there, I won't be a minute,' then she closed the window and disappeared behind the curtains.

I waited. Nothing happened. After a while I strolled over and took a peek in the garage. The red hatchback had been reversed in. I walked round it. Doors and boot were locked. There was a door in the back of the garage that led either into the house or the rear garden. Bare brick walls, concrete floor; no junk or clutter on shelves. I wandered out and waited. I was getting ready to give her a reminder on the bell, when the door opened and she beckoned me inside with a jerk of her head.

'You haven't told me your name.'

'Lomax,' I said. 'Paul Lomax.'

'Go through.' She nodded towards an open door.

I padded over blue-and-gold carpet into a sitting-room that had a blue Dralon sofa and chairs, a big television and a couple of coffee tables with blue leather tops that had gold tooling around the edges. Everything still had the look and smell of newness about it. The walls were emulsioned cream, and there was a reproduction of Van Gogh's *Sunflowers* in a gilt frame on the chimney-breast above a log-effect gas fire.

She sat down on one of the chairs and nodded towards the sofa. The hand with the rings was still holding the red silk of her oriental-style robe tightly around her throat, the other was keeping it together over her knees.

Her pale complexion was clear, unlined, smooth as a baby's. Maybe she'd stumbled on the secret of eternal youth; a Dora Gray who kept a picture of her wrinkled, grey-haired real self locked in the attic. Or maybe she really was well this side of thirty.

I sat facing her. She looked at me warily with green almond eyes. She'd never be beautiful, but she radiated a kind of elemental sexuality; something truly beautiful women often lack. There seemed to be plenty of her under the bathrobe. Tan stockings covered the feet and ankles that were exposed below its hem.

'Where did you say you were from?'

I ignored her question and said, 'I understand you were once married to Rex Saunders.'

She gave me a blank stare, then suddenly smiled and said, 'My older sister was. I'm not married.'

That explained the youthful look. 'Lives here, does she, your sister?'

'She did. We've sold the place. I've stayed on to wind things up.'

'I suppose your sister knows he's dead? Murdered?'

She nodded. Her eyes were suddenly bright and her chin began to quiver. I could tell the words had done something to her. I watched her chewing her lip for a while, then she frowned and said again, 'Where did you say you were from?'

'I'm representing his widow. She asked me to contact his first wife, make sure she knew Mr Saunders was dead and tell her she'd let her know about the funeral arrangements.'

She eyed me warily.

'Could you give me your sister's address?'

'I'm afraid not. She's in London. Moving around, staying at different hotels, flat-hunting. She's going to live there. Until she gets fixed up, I've no idea where she is.' She drew the dressing-gown more tightly around her, looked thoughtful, then said, 'How did you know she lives here?'

'Maintenance payments. Rex Saunders had them sent to this address, monthly.'

She gave me a tight little smile and said, 'Of course.'

I looked at her. I wasn't getting anywhere. She was wary of me. That might not mean anything: an early morning call from a stranger would make any woman wary. I decided to quit the small talk and get down to business. 'There are problems with Rex's estate. I'd hoped your sister might be able to help.'

'Problems?'

'Money problems. A large sum.'

She gave an exasperated snort. 'Really, Mr Lomax, I don't know how you expect my sister to know anything about Rex Saunders's money problems. They've been parted for more than ten years.'

'It's serious, Miss French. A lot of money's gone missing and I've hardly anything to go on. I'm just checking out everyone who was involved with him. Your sister was his first wife, and he was paying her maintenance regularly. Even if she can't help, she might know someone from his past who can.'

'It might be serious to that stuck-up bitch Mona, but it's not serious to me. She's had plenty out of him over the past ten years.'

'I'm not looking for Mrs Saunders's money. This is a large sum he borrowed before he died.'

266

'How large?'

'A million pounds, give or take a few. The surviving creditor is getting edgy about it.'

'Surviving? I don't understand.' Apprehension was colouring the irritation in her voice now.

'Two Barfield businessmen were funding Saunders. One of them was murdered a couple of days ago: a guy called Maslow. You probably read about it in the papers. Two other people were murdered last night. The killer's looking for Saunders's widow and he's looking for me. For that amount of money, Miss French, he'll come looking for *anyone* remotely connected with Rex Saunders.'

The knuckles of the plump little hands that clutched the red silk robe were hard and white. She said, 'You seem to know a lot about this, Mr Lomax. Perhaps you know who murdered Rex.'

'No,' I said softly. 'I don't know who killed Rex Saunders. But I do know that if I don't locate the cash he borrowed, the widow, me, maybe even your big sister, we'll all get pencilled on to somebody's hit list and end up on a mortuary slab.'

'Look, Mr Lomax, I can't talk to you like this. Let me go and put some clothes on, then I'll make coffee and try to work out where my sister's staying at the moment. OK?'

I smiled and nodded.

She stood up, five feet five in her silk stockings, and headed for the door.

'Strange your name being French,' I called after her.

She glanced back. 'I don't know what you mean.'

'Mona told me his first wife was called Pearson: Judy Pearson.'

She treated me to another of her tight-lipped smiles. 'French is my professional name, Mr Lomax. I'm a singer.' And then she gave me a knowing look and said, 'Mona must be more scatterbrained than I thought. My sister's called Joyce Carey.'

She went out. She was as sharp as a tack. She knew I'd been testing her. I heard water pouring from a tap and the clatter of kitchen things; then a door slammed and her feet thudded up the stairs and across the room above me.

I relaxed back and waited. She'd not bothered to open the blue velvet drapes. Maybe she wouldn't want the neighbours to see a man in the house before breakfast. A small chandelier with half a dozen candle-shaped bulbs and not enough lustres to make it interesting was lighting up the room. I let my eyes wander over the blue-and-gold carpet, up the wall to the Van Gogh print, then back to the chair where the impression of her plump little posterior still disturbed the Dralon.

I couldn't hear her walking around any more. A stillness seemed to have settled over the place. I heaved myself out of the chair, went into the hall and yelled 'Miss French?' up a narrow flight of stairs. I didn't get an answer. I heard the whine of a starter, ran back to the window and tugged the drapes aside. The red hatchback was in the middle of the road. She must have free-wheeled it down the hardstanding. She shot me a frightened glance through the sidelight, then the starter whined again.

I kicked a table aside, crashed through to the hall, got the front door open and legged it across the front lawn. The engine was running now. Gears crashed and the car lurched forward. I chased after it. The cold engine wouldn't pull. I caught up and pounded on the boot. Then the car's jerky spluttering smoothed out and she surged away.

I ran back to the Mercedes, slid behind the wheel and left a lot of rubber on the tarmac as I raced down the street after her.

I checked right and left at the intersection with the main road. The long straight stretch to the right was deserted. I turned left, gravel peppered the wheel-arches and the back end slewed as I accelerated hard down the winding lane. A quarter-mile further on, I cleared the bends and overgrown hedges and caught a glimpse of the red car as it approached the crest of a hill and dropped, out of sight, down the other side.

Stockings on under the bathrobe, hair curling the way it does when they've just taken it out of the rollers; I ought to have realized she'd not come to the door straight from her bed: she'd been almost ready to leave.

I forced my anger down into the accelerator pedal and swept over the crest of the rise. I could see her again now, speeding through a village in the trough of the valley. I pressed the pedal into the carpet. Mona's white Mercedes responded. I was closing fast. When I chased her up the far side, I could read the numberplate. As we swept on between the fields beyond, I drew alongside.

I was careering down the wrong side of the road, rear end slewing on shallow bends. I risked a glance at her. She was white-faced and petrified. I pressed the horn, made it blare continuously, began to squeeze her into the verge. I heard a thud, then felt the vibrations as my fender rubbed against her wing. She still didn't slow down. She was clinging on to the wheel, staring straight ahead, mesmerized by the movement, the speed.

And then it was as if someone had grabbed the red car and yanked it back. She must have stood on the brakes. I checked the rear-view mirror. The hatchback was lurching and bouncing over the grass. I pulled up, reversed back, then mounted the verge.

Her door had jammed. She was pushing at it, but it wouldn't budge. I climbed out, waded through grass and nettles and pulled it open for her.

She didn't speak. She half-stepped, half-rolled out of the car, pushed me aside and vomited into the hedge. When she'd finished retching, she turned towards me and gasped, 'You crazy bastard!' The she pressed the frilly white front of her blouse to her chest, leant forward and spat into the grass, trying to clear the taste of vomit from her mouth.

'Feeling better now?' I growled.

'Get lost.'

'Sure,' I said genially. 'But we'll have a talk first. Get back into the car.'

She didn't move, just sagged back against the dented wing and gave me a look like a slap in the mouth. Her going-away outfit was a smart wine-red velvet suit that fitted her a little too well. I guess she'd been wearing it under the robe. She was still gasping for breath. I was catching faint glimpses of something lacy as her heaving breasts kept pressing against the sheer material of the blouse. Without the robe she no longer looked Rubenesque, but she was coming close to plump. I guess the fine-stone merchant had developed a hankering for a little first-class paste. I ran my eyes over her again. Somehow I couldn't find it in me to judge him.

I jerked my thumb towards her car and said, 'Get inside.'

'Get lost.' She put a lot of hate into her voice.

I grabbed her arm, dragged her round and bundled her head-first into the car. One of her shoes fell off. I picked it up, then made to climb in beside her. She scrambled into the passenger seat, showing me a lot of thigh as she hoisted her legs over the gear-stick. I slid behind the wheel, slammed the door to close us in, then turned and grinned at her.

'Where is it?' I said.

'Where's what?'

'The cash. The million quid.'

'You're crazy. Do you know that? Crazy.'

I turned her shoe over in my hand while I tried to think. Wine-red suede with black trim, high heel; the flimsy sole wasn't even scuffed. 'Charles Jourdan, Paris' was impressed in gold on the lining. Her footwear cost foxy old Rex more than I earned most weeks.

I looked at her. The auburn curls were loosening into reddish-brown waves that bunched up on her shoulders. Her perfume was provocative. Maybe the odd half-ounce had cost Rex as much as her shoes.

'Was he generous?' I asked.

'Was who generous?'

'Your sugar daddy, Rex Saunders. He was old enough to be your daddy. You must have thought you were doing your bit for the old-age pensioners.'

'He was my sister's husband, stupid. I hardly remember him.'

I gave her a bored look. 'You don't have a big sister. You were Saunders's mistress. He set you up in the house a couple of years ago, sent you a monthly allowance. Mona made out the cheques. She thought it was maintenance payments to his first wife. She still feels guilty about that.'

I saw a flicker of contempt in her eyes and on her lips. 'Mona made out the cheques?' She sounded surprised.

'Yeah.'

She laughed softly. 'Silly bitch. Rex said she was a repressed, conscience-stricken little cow who'd never come to terms with marrying another woman's husband. She's dead, you know.'

'Who's dead?'

'Rex's first wife. Cancer. About five years ago.'

I looked at her. She seemed to be abandoning the pretence. 'I bet you had him eating out of your hand,' I said.

She gave me a complacent smirk and ran her plump little fingers through the curls. 'He worshipped me,' she said.

'Mona loved him; you were just taking him to the cleaners.'

'Mona made him feel old, inadequate and stupid. I made him feel young, a real man. He more than got his money's worth. And I liked him. I liked him a lot.'

'Talking about money, I want that cash,' I said. 'Either you give it to me, or I'll hand you over to the guys he owed it to. They really would enjoy taking their money's worth.'

'Look, stupid, all I've got is the car, some clothes in the boot and the things I stand up in. I don't even have the cash from the sale of the house. The solicitor still has that.'

'Then why creep out and start doing your Le Mans act all over the countryside?'

'You were frightening me.'

I laughed gently. 'You don't scare that easy.'

I snatched her bag. Under the usual clutter I found a wad of new twenties, about six hundred pounds in all; no bank cards, no bank books. I gave it back to her, then began to search the car. She cajoled, threatened, screamed, threw tearful tantrums in a voice that no longer made any pretence at refinement. I was thorough. Even so, all I found was a couple of hair grips, a comb and some toffee-wrappers.

I took the keys from the ignition, unlocked the boot, lifted out four ivory leather suitcases. I opened them up on the grass, one by one, threw the clothes on to the back seat, then checked the black watered-silk linings. The biggest case was locked. I looked into the car at her and said, 'Keys?'

She didn't answer, but the loathing in her eyes, the poisonous set of her mouth, said it all.

I wrenched the lid open, threw out the dresses and other gear, then slit the lining. She'd done a neat job. An upholsterer couldn't have managed it better. The notes were stitched between two sheets of cotton gauze, the individual piles held in place like cartridges on a gun-belt. A layer of cotton wool padded out the hardness, masked the narrow gaps between the piles. She'd even sprayed perfume over it to hide the smell of so many used notes. I guessed there'd be three or four hundred thousand hidden away there.

'Is this the lot?'

'Of course it's the lot, you thieving bastard.'

'There was more than this. Where's the rest?'

'That's all Rex gave me to take.'

'Take?'

'We were going to Amsterdam. Separately. Rex said we should split the cash. He'd take half, I'd take half.'

'He was walking out on Mona, then?'

'What does it look like?'

I stared at her. Eyes, wintry with defeat, glared back at me.

Her lover's capital had been tied up in deals, a big house and fancy cars. Divorce would have taken time, and Mona would have fought for all she could get. Conning hard cash out of Tulley and Maslow enabled him simply to fade away, to walk off into the sunset with his sexy little playmate. Maybe he'd only hired me on the off-chance I'd dig up some dirt on Mona and cut the cost of a divorce shake-down when it came. Or maybe Mona had been right when she'd said guys who play around are the first to get suspicious and jealous.

'And where did he bank his share of the cash?' I asked.

'He said we couldn't bank it. I stitched what he gave me into the case. He told me he'd hidden his in his office.'

'He must have hidden it well, I couldn't find it. I don't think his creditors did, either, and they smashed the place up.' I heaved the suitcase into Mona's Mercedes.

'What about me?' she wailed.

'Like you said, you've got the car, the clothes, the proceeds from the sale of the house, a lot of beautiful memories.'

I ignored the torrent of abuse, just gave her a genial smile, got behind the wheel of her car and somehow managed to get it back on the road for her before I left with the cash.

After all, I didn't want my shining armour to get too tarnished.

21

I motored along meandering country lanes, moving generally in the direction of Barfield. I needed somewhere safe to stash the cash, and I had to collect Mona then keep out of reach by keeping on the move for a few days.

I pulled off the road, got inside a phone-box in a pub yard and dialled Melody's number.

It didn't ring long. When I told her who it was, she snapped back, 'Oh, it's you, is it?'

'Would you do me a favour, Melody?'

'Favour! Don't you think you should wait until your lady-friend gets out of jail and ask her?' She sounded frosty.

'Jail? I don't follow you.'

'You've not heard the news?'

I said I hadn't, leant against the side of the booth and braced myself.

'It was on breakfast television, would you believe. A white man and a black woman found murdered in a flat on Westfield Avenue. Seems the man's wife got worried when he didn't come home. She thought he might have been in a crash, so she phoned the police. They took the registration number of his car, spotted it behind the flat and went in to check. And guess who owned the place?'

'You tell me.'

'Rex Saunders owned it, as if you didn't know. The police took his widow in for questioning about an hour ago. And where do you think they found her?'

I said I'd no idea.

'Liar. At the bungalow of Barfield private eye, Paul Lomax, where she'd spent the night.' Her tone was as icy as an Eskimo's back yard.

'They mentioned that on television?'

'No, the police told me. Old sex-ray eyes Inspector Mace himself. He was here when I arrived. He's in your office now. He's got a man in the churchyard watching the entrance, and there's another waiting in a car at the back. Mace positively drooled when he gave me the sordid details.'

'What sordid details?'

'The murdered man was a company director who did a little lay preaching and Scout mastering on the side. The black woman was Maslow's maid. And tousle-haired little Mona: oh my!' Melody was injecting an extravagant note of outrage into her voice now.

'What about Mrs Saunders?' I growled.

'Wearing no more than your pyjama jacket

when they turfed her out of your bullet-holed bed. A bullet-holed bed, would you believe! Mace told me they're trying to get the bullets out of your bedroom wall. I always suspected your personal habits were a little bizarre, Paul, but really . . . '

'I can explain.'

'Don't bother.'

I chuckled down the line, then said, 'I'm keeping myself scarce for a few days, Melody.'

'You can keep yourself scarce for a few years, for all I care.'

'Open the mail and answer the phone for me, will you?'

'And what do I say if your lady-friend calls?'

'I don't have a lady-friend. I tried to find myself one the other night, but she gave me the brush-off, remember?'

'What do I say if Miss Pyjama Tops calls?' she hissed.

'Just tell my client I'll be in touch.'

The line went dead. I put down the phone and headed back to the car.

Bedlam had broken out in Barfield, Mona had been grabbed by the cops, and I was planning to high-tail it out of town. I guess my shining armour was almost rusted away.

★ ★ ★

I berthed Mona's white Mercedes in the underground car park beneath the complex of shops and flats where she'd stayed until the Tulleys scared her out.

I'd already deposited the cash at a small suburban branch of a bank where I'd worked with the manager on some credit card fraud. He dealt with me personally, just opened an account in Mona's name and didn't ask the usual questions about money-laundering. I guess he trusted me.

The Tulleys and the guy they called Cripplehead knew now that they'd killed the wrong man. The police had Mona, so she was safe for a while, but I had to clear out fast.

I climbed up to the yard behind the pizza parlour. The Rover was there, just as I'd left it the day before. I strode over and got inside, tucked Mona's car keys into a fold in the upholstery beneath the seat, then started the engine and pulled away. When I turned into the narrow exit alley, I saw it was strewn with up-ended refuse bins and piles of rubbish. I stopped, climbed out and began to clear the mess.

It hit me as I was dragging one of the bins aside. Half an office block, a ten-ton truck: whatever it was, the pain was intense and brief, and oblivion claimed me before my body touched the tarmac.

★ ★ ★

They were staring across at me: six blurred outlines ranged around a trestle table.

I groaned. I must have been doing that for quite a while. I could smell machine oil and felt rough sacking under my cheek. The glimmer of a naked bulb way above the table told me I was in a big, high, corrugated-iron place.

I screwed my eyes up, made them focus, recognized Tulley and his four sons. Old Tulley's glass eye held me in its fixed stare and his sons swarthy faces were expectant, gloating almost.

Behind them, leaning against a column in the shadows, was a slim guy with plenty of blond hair. He was wearing a leather jacket and surgical gauze had been taped to his cheek. One of his hands was bandaged. His body, his face, were perfectly still; his eyes glittering and cold, just like a snake's before it strikes.

When I tried to heave myself into a sitting position, the pain in my shoulder became unbearable. A black tide of nausea swept over me and I fell back on to the sacks. Feet scraped on concrete, hands grabbed me, dragged me up and led me over to the table. I felt a cup touch my lips, then someone started pouring whisky inside me.

'Hey, don't waste good Scotch on that sod.'

They jerked the cup away. The mouthful I'd managed to swallow began to burn inside me. It didn't ease the sickening ache in my shoulder.

'You OK, Lomax?' Old Andrew Tulley asked.

I grunted.

'Does it matter? He's mine now.'

I looked towards the voice, screwed my eyes up, hardened the blurred outline into Jack Tulley's face. Anger and hatred were moulded into every crease and fold.

'You coshed me that night at Saunders's house, then dumped me in the drive,' he said.

'I'd remember a pleasure like that,' I muttered.

'I know it was you, Lomax. We found the papers from Saunders's safe in your bungalow. And a couple of days ago you poked me on the jaw in your office.'

'Yeah,' I said. 'I'll admit that.'

'You're mine now, Lomax.' He repeated the words like a mantra, his thick voice malevolent and gloating.

'I don't think I can let you have him, Jack.'

Six pairs of eyes turned on the blond-haired guy with the Belfast accent. His gaze, cold and strangely remote, was still fixed on me. Professional, detached; nothing stirred behind the scalded flesh of his face.

The distant sound of a motor grew louder until it was idling outside the garage. A horn pipped twice.

'That's Hawkins with the dogs. Let him in,' Andrew Tulley said. He inclined his head towards big sliding doors.

Two sons rose from the table and strode off across the halfacre of oily concrete.

Andrew Tulley's good eye looked from me to Cripplehead, to the son I'd bruised a little, then back to me again. His fleshy lips pulled into a moist, placatory smile. 'Don't argue over him. We'll have a couple of elimination fights, then we'll smear him with blood and put him in the pit with the winning dogs. That way we'll all get to enjoy it.'

'I've a right to some satisfaction first.' Jack sounded sullen.

'I said the dogs can have him for a while. Then our friend here can give him the last rites. That's what we're paying him for.'

'I told you I want him,' the son insisted.

'And I've told you he's going in with the dogs and then the Irishman gets him.'

'You never listen to me. If you had, we'd never have lent that twisting sod Saunders the money in the first place.'

'That's enough.'

Father and son glowered at one another for a long moment, then the son unclenched his fists and lowered his gaze to the food-stained table. While this had been going on, the doors had rolled open and then closed again behind a black Ford van.

Hawkins climbed down from the cab, went round the back and opened the doors. Then Tulley's sons began to help him unload caged dogs. Someone switched on more lights. I made out shelves and work-benches ranged around the walls, gas cylinders, welding gear; the usual tools and salvaged parts that clutter garages. Nearer, in the middle of the expanse of oily concrete, I saw they'd joined together a couple of lorry inspection pits to make a big hole, maybe twenty feet square by four or five deep. Most of the lights were arranged over it, turning it into a bright arena.

I looked back at Andrew Tulley. 'What about the cash Saunders owed you?'

'What about it?' he grunted.

'I've got a lead. Another day, maybe two, and I could recover it.'

Father and sons exchanged amused glances. 'And if we don't treat you rough, let you go on looking, you'll bring it back to us,' Andrew Tulley said.

'That's what Mona Saunders hired me to do.'

'She's dafter than you are, Lomax. We found the cash last night.'

I looked at him. Surprise must have been shining out of my eyes because he grinned and said, 'It was in that fancy summer house, hidden under the floor in an old brass blanket chest.'

I suddenly remembered Mona Saunders telling me about her husband having registered the gazebo as the company office. When he'd told his mistress he'd hidden the cash in his office, that would have been the place he meant, not the small room with the desk at the back of the house.

'You found it all?'

'All he borrowed from us, maybe a little more.'

'Why go on giving Mona Saunders and me all this hassle, if you've found the cash?'

'I couldn't operate if it got round I was a soft touch, Lomax, daft enough to be conned out of half a million quid, too scared to do anything about one of my boys being worked over by some scabby private eye. And I don't like you and Mona Saunders knowing I've got cash that needs laundering. Anyway,' he jerked his head towards Cripplehead, '*he* doesn't love you any more since you gave him the boiling-water treatment. And he's been paid to fix you and I want my money's worth, even if he has shot his way through half the fornicators in Barfield before we got to you.'

Cripplehead didn't like that. For the first time his cold snake's eyes left my face to flicker wounded pride all over Tulley.

'Come on.' Andrew Tulley hoisted me up and led me towards the pit. 'You ought to check out the competition, Lomax. You'll be fighting it off soon.'

I stood at the edge with him and his son Jack. On the far side, concrete steps, sealed at the bottom by crude steel gates, gave on to the sawdust-covered floor of the pit. Hawkins, helped by one of the sons, led the dogs, a pair at a time, down the steps and unleashed them, then crashed the gates shut. The night-black canine obscenities circled one another, slavering and snarling, darting in sudden blurs of movement, huge jaws tearing with a savage ferocity at hairy throats. And after the kills, the victors slobbered ravenously over the shapeless heaps of hot red flesh and black hair.

I gazed around at the sweaty excited faces, the tense bodies and clenched fists; listened to the whistles and cries of encouragement that mingled with the snarls and growling. Once or twice I turned and glanced behind me. Cripplehead was back there in the shadows, hands in pockets, leaning against an iron column, watching and waiting. And beside me, Jack Tulley beat a big bunch of keys against his thigh, jangling out an accompaniment to his shouts and yells.

A bunch of keys, Saunders's last phone call, entries in a diary, snatches of a jilted woman's conversation . . .

I closed my eyes, tried to shut out the sight and sound and smell of it all. Tried to control my pain and fear and impose some order on the thoughts and ideas that were lurching along the panic-blocked alleyways of my mind.

22

Andrew Tulley and son Jack grabbed me, one on either side, dragged me to the rim of the pit and shoved me over. I half jumped, half fell, on to the sawdust.

'Smear him with a carcass, then put Ruby and Jake in,' Andrew Tulley shouted.

Jack Tulley jumped down, grabbed my damaged arm and dragged me to my feet. Through a haze of pain I watched the stocky, balding, barrel-chested Hawkins descend the steps on the far side and come towards me, holding the mangled remains of a dog at arm's length.

I shook Jack Tulley free, backed away until I had him and Hawkins in view, then tried to work a sneer into my voice as I yelled, 'Do you want to know who your wife was really buying the fancy underwear for, Hawkins?'

He stopped dead in his tracks, eyes locked on mine, lips parted, jaw slack.

'You're the jealous type, aren't you, Hawkins? And let's face it, you'd plenty to be jealous about. Couldn't bear even to think of your wife wearing things like that for another man; doing things with him she'd never do with you. She knew how you'd react, of course. That's why she lied when you knocked her around and made her tell you who it was.' I paused to let a wave of pain subside. His eyes were burning into me now. His teeth were clenched. I took a deep breath and began to wind him up some more. 'She can't get enough of it, Hawkins. He's giving it to her in a way you never could. She fancied him so much, she'd do anything rather than risk you maiming or killing him. She lied to you. It wasn't Saunders. If you'd controlled yourself and listened to him that night at the pool instead of killing him with the gun, you might have got the right man and it wouldn't still be going on.'

Hawkins's face was like oily putty. Body hunched, he dropped the ragged carcass, then wiped his mouth with the back of his hand, smearing his cheek with the dog's blood. 'Who is it, Lomax?'

I looked at Jack Tulley, then looked back at Hawkins, and grinned.

'Him?'

'Yeah, him. Jack the lad. Ask him what his long latchkey fits. Don't bother, I'll tell you. It's for a little love-nest in Westfield Avenue. That's where your wife still meets him. Every Thursday afternoon.'

'He's crazy, Ed. Crazy.' Jack Tulley let out a

nervy, snickering laugh and held up his hands in a gesture of protest. 'You can't believe him. You know me. I get all the skirt I want. Why should I fool around with your old lady?'

'If you'd paid a bit less attention to the business and a bit more to the way your partner was letching after your wife, you'd have guessed, Hawkins,' I sneered.

'Shut up,' he snarled at me, then closed in on Jack Tulley, backing him against the wall of the pit.

'It *was* you, wasn't it?' Hawkins croaked. He could hardly choke the words out. His chest was heaving. He suddenly grabbed Tulley by the lapels, savagely butted him in the face and screamed, 'Wasn't it?' then slid huge, hairy hands around his throat and squeezed and shook.

Andrew Tulley and his other three sons leapt down into the pit and began to kick and punch Hawkins, struggling to drag him off.

I ran over the blood-splattered sawdust and staggered up the steps on the far side. Dogs were yelping and snarling, hurling themselves against the heavy mesh of the cages, excited to a frenzy by the violent action. I pulled up the bolts that secured the doors, setting the dogs free to help the pandemonium along.

I heard a crack and a clang as a bullet punched its way through a corrugated-iron wall behind me. I glanced up, looked across the pit and into the shadows beyond, saw the Irish hitman taking aim. Crouching low, I scurried between the machinery, trying to get to the van.

Bullets thudded into benches, tore through metal walls as I tugged at the van door and climbed inside. I got down below the dash, switched on the ignition and got the engine going. I risked a glance through the windscreen and saw Cripplehead running towards me, aiming the gun. I ducked. The screen shattered. I revved the engine, crashed the gears into reverse and accelerated hard towards the big doors. The impact noise was deafening, but the metal held. I shoved the gear-stick over, kept my head down and hurtled back towards the pit. I heard a crash and the yelping of frantic dogs as the fender hit some cages, then I reversed hard to give the doors another battering. They held, the engine stalled, the cab door slid back and I was staring at the hired killer. When he brought up the gun, I froze.

And then he reeled back, the slobbering jaws of a noise-crazed dog locked on his thigh. I swung my legs from under the wheel, aimed a kick that contacted with his throat, then dropped from the cab.

The big doors had been forced off their

tracks. I managed to squeeze through a gap between the frame and the buckled sheeting, then staggered off into the night, weaving drunkenly between the lines of scrapped cars, trying to find my way back to the road and some law and order.

23

Summer was lingering on, soft and golden, but through the open window a faint breeze was ushering in the promise of rain, a hint of autumn. I rested my arm on the desk and took the weight off the sling. Barfield General's resident bone-setter, a white-coated guy with clammy hands and halitosis, had diagnosed a fractured collar-bone, prescribed painkillers and told a nurse to strap me up.

I'd flushed the painkillers down the pan and was nuzzling my way through my second four-finger life-saver when I heard the genteel tapping on the inner door. I pushed my glass between the piles of papers and called out, 'Come on in.'

Mona Saunders came towards me across the threadbare carpet. Vivian had been busy. Her almost-black hair was drawn tightly back, sleek and shining, and gathered into a bun at the nape of her neck. Her big eyes had been discreetly made up; her lips tinted a brownish-pink that was so near their natural colour it had almost been a waste of time. The black dress had tight sleeves, wide padded shoulders, a high neckline and a hem that was maybe an inch above the knee. It looked as if it had cost plenty, and she was giving it plenty of shape. Black stockings and plain high-heeled shoes that seemed to be made of black glass gave it the finishing touches. I guess it was her idea of widow's weeds.

'You've hurt your arm,' she said.

'Writer's cramp,' I said.

She raised her eyebrows.

'I've been making out your bill.'

She gave me a tolerant little smile that was meant to tell me a mature adult like her would find humour like mine pathetic, then sat down on a red plastic chair, legs pressed neatly together, hands wrapped around a small black patent-leather handbag that didn't have a strap.

'I guessed something had happened when the police let me go. They told me you'd phoned them. It's all over now, isn't it?' She was begging for it to be all over in that soft refined voice.

'Yeah, it's all over, Mrs Saunders.'

'And those men, that Cripplehead creature, they won't come pestering us any more?'

'When they get out they'll be too old to pester your pet canary.'

She shivered. 'What did the police arrest them for?'

'The Tulleys beat Hawkins to death. When the police arrived, they were burying him at the back of the scrap yard.'

'You mean the man called Hawkins with the farm down the lane?'

'The very same. One of Tulley's sons was having an affair with Hawkins's wife. Hawkins tried to take a little retribution and the Tulleys got too rough when they dragged him off.'

'And my husband, who killed him?'

'Hawkins. He guessed his wife was having an affair and tried to beat the name of the guy out of her. She told him it was your husband to protect her lover.'

'Was Rex . . . ?'

I gave her a steady look. 'She was lying, Mona. I know for sure she was lying.'

'And the money Rex borrowed?'

I didn't see much point in tarnishing beautiful memories of her loving union with foxy old Rex. So I said, 'Tulley told me he'd recovered his. The cash Maslow lent your husband was sown into the lining of a suitcase. It's in a bank account now, in your name.' I groped for my wallet, took out the manager's receipt and refreshed my memory. 'Four hundred and thirty-two thousand.' I slid the paper across the desk. She picked it up and gazed at it with those huge eyes.

I fished keys and a car park check-out card from a desk drawer and passed them over. 'Your car's in the parking bay under the shopping precinct. The front nearside wing's been scraped a little. I'm sorry about that.'

'Where did you find it: the money, I mean?'

'The gazebo your husband registered as an office. The Tulleys found theirs under the floor. The suitcase was amongst some junk in a corner. They must have thought it was empty when they searched the place.'

'I suppose I ought to hand it over to the police,' she said.

'All you'll get is more hassle. I'd leave it for a while, then get some good advice about investing it. If the police start asking stupid questions, say it's money Rex put aside for you. Don't say any more. They can't prove it's not legitimate, because Maslow's dead.'

'But it's not mine. It belongs to Maslow's family.'

'Did he have any family?' I asked. 'If he did, they wouldn't thank you for handing it over to the police and inviting them to start poking their noses into his affairs. You've lost your husband, you've had your house wrecked, you've been traumatized. Look on it as compensation.'

She rose, came close to the desk and gazed down at me for a moment, then snapped open the handbag, picked up the keys and card and slipped them inside.

I figured I might as well submit my account for services rendered before she walked out of my life for ever, so I passed the sheet of paper over the desk.

She glanced at it, took a chequebook and pen from her bag and sat down again. She crossed her legs, rested the handbag on her knee and used it to support the chequebook while she wrote. She'd given the crimson nail varnish a miss. Without it, the slender hands emerging from tight black sleeves looked almost childlike.

She ripped out the cheque, folded it, returned to the desk and laid it on the blotter.

'Thanks,' I said.

'No. Thank *you*, Paul. I owe you a very great deal.'

I smiled at her over the heaps of papers, trying to hide my embarrassment. Asking for money never comes easy; asking women is the worst.

'Did you manage to contact Rex's first wife?'

This was something else she didn't need to know the truth about. 'She died, about a month ago,' I said. 'You don't need to send any more of those maintenance payments.'

Mona seemed shocked. 'That's awfully sad.

We never met, but I never stopped feeling bad about her.'

The pain in my shoulder had got worse. I leant back in the chair, trying to get more comfortable. 'Ten years is a long time and, like you said, things were over between them long before you came on the scene.'

'Rex's funeral's this afternoon,' she said softly. 'Some friends from the bridge club are coming and Vivian said he'd make the numbers up. As far as I know, Rex didn't have any family, and the only person he was really close to was me, so there won't be anyone else.'

She gazed down at me. Maybe she was inviting me along, too. I tried to make some sense of the mysterious lights that were shining deep in her eyes. After what seemed like quite a while, she murmured, 'Thanks, Paul.'

'It's only what you hired me for.'

She shook her head. 'I don't mean that. I mean thanks for the other night: the night we spent together. I . . . I'll always be grateful to you.'

I must have looked mystified, because she began to colour up as she went on, 'For not making love to me. It was very obvious that you wanted to, but you didn't and . . . '

The words faded away beneath the rumble

of traffic coming in from the street and she looked down at her hands. I could feel my cheeks burning, too. She didn't have to mention something as intimate as that. It was an experience we both had to forget.

She brought her eyes back to mine. 'Why, Paul? Why didn't you make love to me? You must have known that I wanted you to.'

I gazed up at her, at the almost too perfect face and the beautiful body in that elegant dress. After a dozen heartbeats I said softly, 'We were in the room and in the bed I used to share with my wife.'

Her eyes brightened with understanding and her mouth shaped into a soundless, 'Oh.'

'What happens after the funeral?' I was trying to jump the conversation on to fresh tracks.

'I've put the house up for sale and I'm going to London.'

'Back to modelling?'

'I no longer have the look.'

'Guys in the modelling business all like Vivian, are they? You look pretty sensational to me.'

She laughed and showed me the dimples in her cheeks. 'You know, Paul, you can be shocking and sweet at the same time. I'm too old. And no, they're not all like Vivian. Some of them are almost as red-blooded as you.'

'What then, if it's not modelling?'

'I'm going into a convent: Sisters of Mercy.'

My jaw must have dropped a yard at that, because she laughed some more and said, 'Do you have to look so surprised? I'm just going to stay there for a few weeks. Try and find myself again. If it begins to mean something to me, I might not leave.'

She laughed again when she held out her hand. 'Don't look so shocked, Paul. I'm beginning to feel a little offended.'

Her hand was like a child's in mine. Shaking it seemed a stupidly formal gesture between two adults who'd spent the night almost naked in one another's arms.

'I've promised Vivian I'll write and let him know how I'm getting on.' She moved towards the door, then looked back. 'I hope things go well for you with your friend downstairs. If you ever want to look me up, Vivian will have my address. But if I decide to stay on in the convent, it might be better if you didn't.' She gazed at me in silence for a few seconds, then turned and headed for the stairs.

I eased myself into a more comfortable position and groped for the glass I'd hidden between the piles of papers. After a couple of sips I tried to picture Mona in her nun's habit. It all seemed a little surreal, the sort of thing you'd conjure up after a two-bottle bender, and I abandoned the effort. Her cheque was on the blotter. I unfolded it and saw she'd more than quadrupled the figure I'd had in mind.

The faint sound of women's voices, cool and reserved, floated up from the stairs. Then feet pattered across the outer office and Melody breezed in, blue eyes flashing, two spots of colour burning on her cheeks.

'I've just met your lady friend, Little Miss Pyjama Tops, on the landing. Wearing Louis Vuitton today. It's nice to see she's not been left destitute.' Melody's voice was icy.

'Vuitton?' I looked blank.

'The dress: it was on the cover of last month's *Vogue*.'

'I thought it was one of her mother's old frocks. It had a kind of sixties look about it.'

'You'd like that, wouldn't you, Paul: little Mona in a Sixties outfit, pelmet skirt no lower than your pyjama jacket? Anyway, what do I care what your bedmates wear?'

'Client,' I corrected. 'Not bedmate. I don't have a bedmate.'

'Client, bedmate, I imagine it's all the same to you.' She stood in the middle of the carpet, hands on hips, blonde curls piled up: dress, shoes, lipstick and nails the same vibrant red.

I grinned across at her. Mona had really

got under her skin.

'Do you want me to have lunch brought in, or has Mona dashed back to the bungalow to rustle up something tasty for two?'

'She's going to her husband's funeral. Then she's heading south to take up the veil. She's going into a convent.'

Melody looked almost as surprised as I had.

'You're kidding?'

I shook my head. 'Sisters of Mercy.'

She relaxed a little and began to smile. 'What did you do to her, Paul? One night of love with you and she's legging it for the cloisters.'

'She was very devout. Had a strict Catholic upbringing in Ireland. And they don't come much stricter than that.'

Melody's smile broadened. 'Rebuffed you, did she?'

I sniffed. 'Mrs Saunders was a client. She didn't have any cause to rebuff me.'

'By the way, Chief Inspector Sloane called. He wanted you to phone him as soon as you got in.'

'I suppose he's going to tell me about my award.'

'Award?'

'Finding Saunders's murderer, turning in a hitman: maybe they're going to give me the freedom of the borough?'

'The only repeatable words I heard were 'perverting the course of justice' and 'I'll crucify that conniving so-and-so'.'

I grinned. 'There's gratitude.'

Melody came up close, leant over the desk, propping herself on her arms. 'Fragrantly spectacular' were the only words that came to mind at the time.

'Lunch, Paul: do you want something brought in?'

I rested my good arm on the blotter. Our faces were almost kissing-distance now and I noticed, for the first time, that her eyes were flecked with green and gold. They were very bright. Her smile widened and she began to giggle.

'What's so funny?'

'I don't know. It just comes over me when I think you're getting amorous.' She was almost laughing now.

'What's funny about me being amorous? Anyway, I'm being serious, not amorous.'

'We've been over this, Paul. I'm not sure I like serious.'

'Why don't we bunk off for the afternoon? You can drive us to Ramford, we could dine at Luigi's, and then go on from there.'

'I was with you until you said 'go on from there'.'

'I'm talking about starting at the beginning again, not picking up where we left off. You never know, you might get to like serious.' I moved my face closer.

She giggled and pushed herself off the desk. 'OK, cheeky, let's bunk off together. With your arm in the sling, I should be fairly safe.'

I pushed myself up, pocketed Mona's cheque, and offered Melody my good arm.

I let her move ahead when we went down the stairs. When she reached the landing, she paused and looked up at me. 'If you're serious about being serious, Paul, there's a little four-letter word a woman likes to hear.'

I pretended to be mystified, then asked brightly, 'Is it 'please'?'

She sighed and gave me a look of utter resignation. 'That's six, Paul. Six letters, not four. I'm spending the afternoon with a one-armed emotional illiterate who can't even count.'

We do hope that you have enjoyed reading this large print book.

Did you know that all of our titles are available for purchase?

We publish a wide range of high quality large print books including:
Romances, Mysteries, Classics
General Fiction
Non Fiction and Westerns

Special interest titles available in large print are:
The Little Oxford Dictionary
Music Book
Song Book
Hymn Book
Service Book

Also available from us courtesy of Oxford University Press:
Young Readers' Dictionary
(large print edition)
Young Readers' Thesaurus
(large print edition)

For further information or a free brochure, please contact us at:
Ulverscroft Large Print Books Ltd.,
The Green, Bradgate Road, Anstey,
Leicester, LE7 7FU, England.
Tel: (00 44) 0116 236 4325
Fax: (00 44) 0116 234 0205